For Young People

The Blue Man
Big Max
Mystery of the Missing Moose
The Boy Who Could Make Himself Disappear
Sinbad and Me
Mystery of the Witch Who Wouldn't
Hey, Dummy
Chloris and the Creeps
Chloris and the Freaks
Chloris and the Weirdos
The Terrible Love Life of Dudley Cornflower
Headman
The Doomsday Gang
Run for Your Life
Dracula, Go Home!
The Ape Inside Me

For Adults

The Pushbutton Butterfly
The Kissing Gourami
Dead As They Come
A Pride of Women
The Giant Kill
The Princess Stakes Murder
Matchpoint for Murder
The Body Beautiful Murder
The Screwball King Murder

THE GHOST OF HELLSFIRE STREET

KIN PLATT

DELACORTE PRESS/NEW YORK

To Olga Litowinsky

Published by
Delacorte Press
1 Dag Hammarskjold Plaza
New York, N.Y. 10017

Manufactured in the United States of America

First printing

Designed by Jack Ellis

Library of Congress Cataloging in Publication Data

Platt, Kin.
  The ghost of Hellsfire Street.
  SUMMARY: Steve Forrester, the only witness to a kidnapping
that doesn't seem to have occurred, sorts through a medley of
clues to solve a mystery in his Long Island town.
  [1. Mystery and detective stories.   2. Kidnapping—
Fiction.   3. Ghost stories]   I. Title.
PZ7.P7125Gh   [Fic]   80-10446

ISBN 0-440-02795-0

ISBN 0-440-02796-9 lib. bdg.

Contents

Part Two

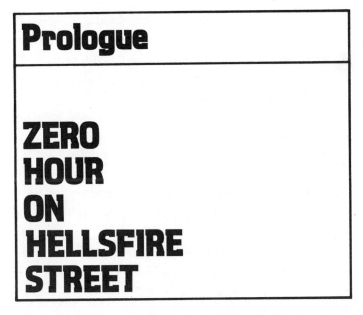

Prologue

ZERO HOUR ON HELLSFIRE STREET

From where I stood on the high bleak bluff, the winter night wind hit me in icy gusts, tearing my breath away, chilling my bones. Far below, the dark waters of Jonah's Bay swished and broke on the rocky shore. The yellow moon hung high in the sky, full and bright.

Slanted behind the desolate cliff was a thin straggly stand of pines serving as a windbreak to the old house on Hellsfire Street. It was a Garrison Colonial dating back to the year 1700. It was called the Old King Dick house. When some clouds drifted across the moon, I ran for its protective shadows.

Herky had warned me about this house, that its name had a special meaning, spelling out danger. But I had to get inside without being seen. Old Mrs. Teska's life depended on that. She didn't have any other friends in town to look after her but Sinbad and me.

I had explained it all to Sinbad before I took off, telling him why he couldn't come along. It was to be a secret night mission. No dogs allowed. Not even tough English bulls. Sinbad didn't think much of my excuse. He likes excitement and adventure.

I couldn't tell Sheriff Landry that I was doing this, or why, because he would have grounded me. Kids aren't supposed to do superspy work. And I was giving him enough of a headache already because I was the only witness to a kidnapping. Only I couldn't prove the man had disappeared, and nobody else even believed he was gone.

So I had to get some facts on that, and help Mrs. Teska, and convince Sheriff Landry that some crooks were plotting to get his job. He didn't pay any attention to that idea, either.

Dark Cloud, the old Shinnecock medicine man, who had the shaman gift of prophecy, of seeing into the future, agreed I had a problem. He told me how I was facing great danger. Also, that the Great Spirit couldn't help me with this, and that I had to go ahead with the strength of my own spirit to see me through.

That wasn't such terrific good news from my viewpoint. Then he added that I had to go through the fire. And I had to listen to the wind.

I didn't have the heart to tell Dark Cloud I was chicken about fire. But he must have known that, because he gave me his own spirit bag for good luck. Inside it were the very special things Dark Cloud used for his magic.

What Dark Cloud didn't tell me was how I was supposed to use them.

The pirate ghost was another problem. He told me what he wanted me to do. I didn't think I could do it, and that made it a bigger problem.

How do you argue with a ghost?

I thought the prayer room of the old Colonial on Hellsfire would be the right place for resolving all these things I couldn't handle.

But, as it turned out, that prayer room proved to be the most dangerous place of all.

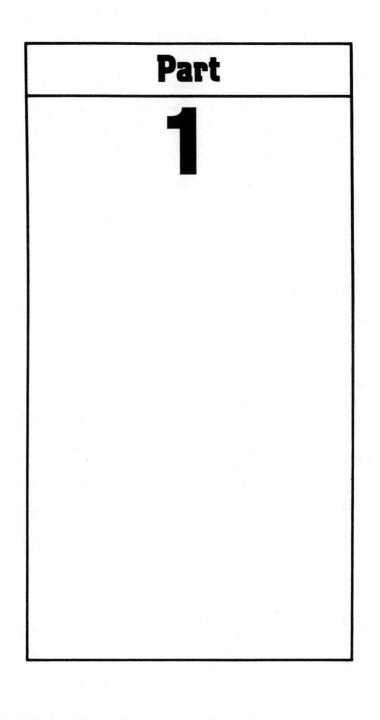

Part

1

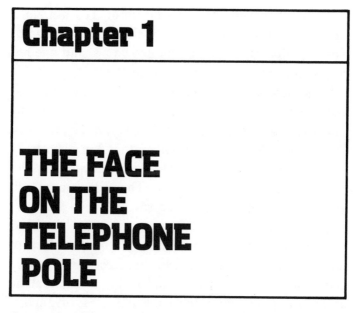

Chapter 1

THE FACE ON THE TELEPHONE POLE

Our town of Hampton is on the northeast tip of Long Island, off the bay. Summers are pleasant, but winters are fierce, so cold that at times you feel your blood is freezing and your body turning to stone.

The trees were nearly bare now, and winter was on its way. The wind swept across the bay, knifing through my squall coat, chilling my knees, freezing my ears, turning my hands blue. I was out walking my bulldog Sinbad.

He shuffled along Steamboat Road with his waddling gait, not bothered by the biting wind, sniffing at the dry leaves blowing around, taking his time.

English bulldogs aren't afraid of anything. So they don't worry and they don't hurry. It's their good nature.

I shook his heavy leash. "Hurry it up, you big ape. I'm freezing to death."

Sinbad is so ugly that he's beautiful. His muzzle is dark, his coat a light brindle, his thick neck a blaze of white like his paws. He has one brown eye and one red eye, with a stripe of white between them.

He looked back up at me with his crooked grin, as if asking what was the hurry. Then he kept plodding along, following each new scent, ignoring me, as usual. I've never really convinced Sinbad that I'm his master.

He stopped at one of the old timber telephone poles on the street, sniffing around. Then he backed off, looked up, shook his head, and sneezed.

"Gesundheit!" I said. "Come on already. It's cold."

I snapped the leash but he didn't budge. He kept staring up at the thick pole, his head cocked. Then he made the strange cracked sound in his throat that he uses to ask a question. He sounds like a parrot, then. I followed his gaze upward.

"It's only a poster. Some kind of advertising. We got no time for reading junk. Do something, will you?"

Sinbad scowled darkly, looking very tough and stubborn. He's like a little kid and wants things explained. Usually I keep him informed about what's happening, and he pays close attention. But I was so cold now, my teeth were chattering. All I wanted to do was go home and get warm.

I started away but Sinbad didn't budge. When the leash drew tight, his weight jarred my arm. Moving him when he isn't willing is like trying to pull an army tank.

He made the throaty sound again, his eyes fixed on the small white poster. "Okay, I'll read it," I said, "and then you got to do what we came out for. No more stalling around."

Sinbad whined and wagged his stub of a tail.

"Okay, then. It's a deal."

It was a glossy white poster taped to the pole at eye level. At the top was a photo of a man's face. Underneath, it read in thick black type: VOTE FOR BRADLEY CASE FOR SHERIFF.

At the bottom in smaller letters was: CITIZENS' COMMITTEE FOR A CLEANER COUNTY.

"It's nothing," I told Sinbad, "like I told you. Some jerk I never heard of is running for sheriff."

Sinbad scowled, his red eye turned up at me angrily. A rumbling growl sounded deep in his throat. It surprised me, and then I realized what I had just told him. Stunned, I turned to look at the poster again.

I had never heard of this guy Bradley Case who was running for sheriff. I didn't recognize his picture. He looked young. A jutting chin, long nose, thin mouth, dark eyes, dark hair.

I didn't know anything about a Citizens' Committee for a Cleaner County, either. I didn't know Hampton needed any cleaning up.

I knew we already had a sheriff. Langwell Otis Landry was his full name. Not only was he sheriff and police chief, but he happened to be a good friend of my dad's, and also of Sinbad and me.

There wasn't any crime rate in Hampton. No gambling. Nobody getting ripped off that I knew about. Sheriff Landry had kept it that way since he took office, about fifteen years ago, before I was born.

Another thing I didn't know was that he had to run again for office. I was so used to Sheriff Landry being the top lawman of our district, I had taken it for granted that the job would always be his.

Sinbad was pressing his hard head against my leg, and now he whined up at me. "Okay, I'll tell you what the poster says," I said. "But don't get mad. Remember, it was your own idea to find out."

I explained about this new group putting up somebody to take over Sheriff Landry's job. Politics was something I didn't know very much about, and I never paid any attention to it. I just barely understood how it worked.

"It doesn't mean this new guy will get it," I told Sinbad. "He's just running for the office. Maybe this same thing has been going on all the time, and I never knew it. They try to put new guys in, and the Hampton people still like Sheriff Landry, and vote him right back into his job."

Sinbad sniffed and hooked his twin lower tusks outside his upper lip. With his thrust-out jaw, he looks awfully menacing. He happens to be gentle, although he is strong enough to wreck anybody or anything. He's bigger than the average English bull, like his father Prince John was, and much more powerful than his weight of sixty pounds suggests.

I thought he understood now that Sheriff Landry didn't have to worry over his job, and started walking away. The jarring jolt in my arm told me Sinbad wasn't convinced.

I shot him an annoyed look. "Come on, I thought

you understood. Sheriff Landry will win easy. Most people here never heard of this Bradley Case."

Sinbad looked up at me, then pointed his dark muzzle up to the poster. He made the cracked-voiced parrot sound.

"Oh," I said. "Excuse me. I see what you mean."

I reached up and pulled the poster off. Sinbad yawned and sighed contentedly. He moved away from the pole now without any more urging. He's always more reasonable when I take his advice.

"That was a good idea, Sinbad," I said. "One less poster for this Bradley Case means one more vote for Sheriff Landry."

I had an idea Sheriff Landry would be real pleased when he found out he had two good friends like Sinbad and me trying to help him get reelected to office. Maybe he didn't know about the new competition. I couldn't wait to tell him.

Chapter 2

MYSTERY OF THE MAN WITHOUT AN OVERCOAT

After Sinbad had his walk, I took him back down the hill to our house, and fed him. Then I remembered my mom had asked me to pick up a few things at Mrs. Teska's grocery store so she wouldn't have to go shopping when she got home from work. Milk, eggs, butter, and bread.

I told Sinbad to watch the house, and took off on my bike, figuring it would be faster than walking in the wind. But when I got to her store, I was surprised to see Mrs. Teska had the blue card in the window that said: CLOSED. I tried the door in case she had put the sign in backward by mistake, but it was locked. I peered in through the glass door but it was closed, all right. Mrs. Teska wasn't there, and she runs the place herself.

There's another store a couple of blocks farther

down Steamboat Road and I headed for it. Mrs. Teska has to take off at times during the day, to go to her bank, or see her doctor, so I wasn't worried. I see her nearly every day on my way to school, and we're old friends. She once saved Sinbad's life. Some nut poisoned him when he was a young puppy, and Mrs. Teska fed him a healing potion she remembered from her farmland in Europe, and he recovered. Naturally, she's his friend, too.

I picked up the groceries at the other store. The return trip was uphill and into the wind, a lot harder. I was riding the sidewalk, carrying the bag against my chest, leaning on the pedals of my ten-speed bike, head down, trying to be streamlined.

A sudden shifting gust of wind sweeping down from the bay a few miles north nearly blew me off my bike. I had to stop in the middle of a driveway, and looked up from force of habit. There are a lot of great old estates in Hampton, some hidden along back streets, and in my neighborhood I know most of the people from the days when I had my newspaper delivery route. This was the house of Gunther Waldorf. He's one of the more famous people in our town, a scientist who writes books on ecology. I used to collect for the newspapers at the end of the week, and I had spoken to him several times. His accent was North European, and he was a distant kind of man, polite but reserved.

A car engine cranked over and revved up loudly. It was almost dusk, and as I looked down the long gravel driveway, I saw a man between two bigger men. He looked to be off-balance, as if they were dragging him. They wedged him into the car and slammed the back door. The car was into gear and moving instantly, scattering the gravel as it zoomed down the driveway, coming straight at me.

I had been gawking, straddling my bike, waiting for the wind to die down. Now with the grade and wind, I had trouble getting up enough speed to pedal out of the driveway. The car came roaring up as if the driver never saw me. His headlights weren't on. At the last moment, I managed to swerve out of the way.

The car was a big black Continental. Besides nearly running over me, it almost made me drop my bag of groceries. The driver was up to me now and I yelled at him. "Slow down, you dope! You nearly killed me!"

His window was closed, and his eyes were set straight ahead. He spun his wheel sharply left, and the big car spit gravel and fishtailed onto Steamboat Road.

I saw three men on the backseat. Two big guys wearing dark overcoats, and between them a white-haired man wearing steel-rimmed glasses. His eyes were closed, and his lips were moving. I hadn't seen him for some time, but I recognized Gunther Waldorf.

The big car roared away up the street. The driver hit his brakes at the next corner, took a sharp right turn, and disappeared from sight.

After I got my breath back I wondered why the driver was in such a big hurry. Then I remembered Gunther Waldorf in the back seat, and wondered why he wasn't wearing an overcoat on such a cold day.

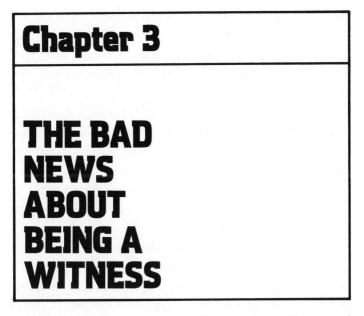

Chapter 3

THE BAD NEWS ABOUT BEING A WITNESS

Sheriff Landry is tall. Six feet three inches of bone and muscle with something wolflike about his gaunt face and yellow eyes.

He looked down at me. "Kidnapping, you say?"

"Yes, sir. Except that it wasn't a kid but—"

His waving hand cut me short. "It applies to a child or adult. Gunther Waldorf, you said?"

"Right, Sheriff. He was in between these two big guys and—"

He interrupted impatiently. "Do you have any idea who Gunther Waldorf is, Steve?"

"Yes, sir. He's the same man I used to deliver my newspaper to when I had that route a couple years ago."

His yellow eyes blazed hotly, and I thought Sheriff Landry was going to blast me. Instead he rubbed the sour look off his face and began smiling. "It's crazy," he said as if talking to himself. "I've known this boy since he was born. I've heard how he thinks too many times. So why should I let him give me an ulcer or a heart attack now?"

"Are you feeling okay, Sheriff?" I asked.

He took a deep breath and let it out slowly with a sigh. "Never better. Now you were saying about Mr. Waldorf—?"

"I meant that I knew him from my paper route as just another subscriber and customer before I found out he was this famous ecologist."

Sheriff Landry nodded, relaxing his lips. "Good boy. I ought to know how you set me up, by now. Now if I understand you correctly—and I wouldn't bet on it— you're telling me two men took Mr. Gunther Waldorf from his house on Tupelo Lane into a car waiting in his driveway. Correct?"

"Well, actually there were three, if you want to count the creep driving, who nearly ran me over."

He threw out his big hands, his face muscles twitching under his tight skin. "Okay, we'll count him, too. But only two men had him, were dragging him into the car against his will?"

"Yes, sir." I looked at the staircase leading up from the living room, wondering why his daughter Minerva hadn't come downstairs yet to poke holes in my story. She's even better at it than her old man sometimes.

"You can prove, of course, that they were dragging him against his will. I mean, Mr. Waldorf shouted something at you to that effect, right? That he was in the process of being abducted, kidnapped."

"Well, no, not exactly, Sheriff. It looked like they were dragging him because he was leaning forward too far. Nobody walks that way."

"I hadn't thought much about that," he said. "Any other way you could assume he was being kidnapped, other than the extreme angle at which you saw him leaning?"

"Yeah. He wasn't wearing his overcoat."

The room seemed too quiet. I could hear the refrigerator motor running in the kitchen, the oak floor boards creaking under the Sheriff's feet. The wind rattled the wood shutters outside the windows.

Sheriff Landry rubbed his lower lip with his thumb. "In other words, if he had been wearing an overcoat, you wouldn't be telling me all this now?"

"Right, Sheriff. You know how cold it gets around here. Everybody else, even the driver, wore an overcoat. I figured they had to be cold-blooded killers to be in such a hurry that they wouldn't wait until he put his overcoat on."

He jammed his hands on his hips. His voice sounded hoarser. "Any other reasons for your assuming the men were cold-blooded killers? Were they waving knives and guns, shooting their way out of Waldorf's house, cutting up his servants?"

"Well, no, I didn't see any of that. But the driver came straight at me full speed not giving me a chance to get out of the way with my bike."

His wolflike eyes glowed hotly. "So he hit you with that big car, knocked you flying, ran right over you and killed you?"

"Oh, come on, Sheriff. You know what I mean. He

didn't try to ease up at all, hit his brakes, or even blow his horn warning me he was coming. If I hadn't managed to get out of the way in the last second, he would have hit me. I'm not kidding. He zoomed down that driveway doing fifty at least. If another car had been coming down Steamboat Road then, you would have had a lot of dead bodies out there to count."

He snapped his long fingers. "No question about it, my luck is holding up. Now do you happen to know what's behind this dastardly plot? Any reason you can think of for anybody to be kidnapping an important man like Gunther Waldorf?"

"Well, kind of—"

"You do know what an ecologist is, don't you?"

"Yes, sir. They worry a lot about things happening to our environment. Like the smog in the air and rotten water and—"

"Fine. That's what they do. It's important work these days, and Mr. Waldorf happens to be one of the foremost in his field.

"Now tell me your theory about why he was kidnapped. I just want to make sure I get it all down right, so we can plan our countermoves correctly, Steve."

It seemed to me that Sheriff Landry was being too careful this time about getting all the facts. If I'd had the job, I would have been on the horn long since, getting roadblocks out on that black Lincoln Continental. I would have sent out the P.D. helicopters to check below for four men in a speeding car, one without an overcoat. Since we're right off the bay, I'd have asked the Coast Guard for a little help, too, a fast cutter to look around for any small boats running out to sea.

Sheriff Landry was getting impatient waiting for an answer, and I suddenly realized I didn't have a real good one. I shoved my hands into my squall coat and the folded piece of paper inside my pocket seemed to be the right answer. I unfolded it and handed it to him.

"What's this?" he asked, taking it.

"I found it on a telephone pole down near Mrs. Teska's store," I said. "I think they're behind it."

"Who?" he said. I pointed to the bottom part.

He read the lines on the poster slowly, and stared at me. "The Citizens' Committee?"

"Partly. You didn't notice what else it said. About this guy Bradley Case running for your office."

He shook his head as if tired. "I'm not sure I'm getting all this. Are you suggesting Bradley Case had Gunther Waldorf kidnapped?"

"No, but you asked for my theory. Who is this guy Bradley Case anyway?"

"Apparently he's running for the office of sheriff," Sheriff Landry said with a thin smile.

"How come? Aren't you doing a good job?"

He grunted. "That's not up to me to say, but for the people who live around here. That's why they have elections for office every couple of years, Steve. Just in case they got the wrong man in, and so they get another chance and can throw him out."

I pointed to the bottom line of the glossy paper. "It says here *For a Cleaner County*—is ours dirty?"

"Not that I know of," he said. "But it wouldn't hurt if things were cleaned up here and there. Sure, I'd go along with that."

"Maybe you don't know it, Sheriff," I said, "but a lot of new people have been moving into Hampton lately. Some of them never heard of you, and all the good work you did, I bet."

He nodded. "It's possible, so what?"

"So what? So if they don't know you, and they see posters all over town to vote for this Bradley Case, he can beat you out of your job."

"That's right, Steve. Part of the democratic process. The people have the right to vote for their preference. In this country, anyway. That's why it's an important right to have."

"What if he's a jerk—doesn't know anything about it?"

Sheriff Landry shrugged his wide shoulders. "Doesn't matter," he barked. "If he gets enough support, he gets elected. For all you know, he might be good, too."

"Gee, Sheriff, the way you talk, it sounds like you don't care if this guy Bradley Case beats you for office."

He stuck his long forefinger out toward my nose. "What I care has nothing to do with it, Steve. The people of the town decide. If enough of them want Case and vote for him, he's got the job. Simple as that."

I shook my head dumbly, unable to think of anything to say.

He glared down at me. "Sorry, but you're dead wrong here. I know all about the new people moving in. The new houses, the new condominiums. People are moving out of the big cities, retiring on Long Island. Or some don't mind the travel time as long as they have a better place to live and bring up their kids. That's progress."

"Okay, but they still don't know anything about how this town works," I said.

"Then they'll find out," he said tersely. "Still part of the democratic process. The voters decide. Last year you were flunking science, as I recall. Now it seems to me as if you're not paying enough attention to your social studies, government, and so on."

"Okay," I said, "maybe you're right, and I'm going to study up on that, Sheriff. But you wanted to hear my theory, right? About the kidnapping?"

He glanced at his watch. "So far I haven't heard a thing."

"Then listen to this," I said, pointing to the white poster in his hand. "They say they're for a cleaner county, and I still haven't heard we got a dirty one. So they're telling a lie, right off the bat.

"I bet once they get people here to think they really need a cleaner county and vote them in, they're going to do just the opposite. They're going to take over the beaches, and use them for digging oil, and making money instead of letting the people enjoy them. They'll foul up our water and oyster beds with oil spills and like that. They're going to do a lot of rotten things all over because Hampton will trust them."

I'd heard of things like that happening.

"And to make sure they can get away with it," I went on, "they decided to get Gunther Waldorf out of the way now, because he would be just the guy to see what they were up to, and write about it and make a big stink about it." I hadn't thought about all that, but as I heard my words, they made sense to me.

He stood shaking his head, his thin lips working. Then he said, "It's my own fault for asking." He headed abruptly for the door with long strides, and I went after him. He pulled on his squall coat, and strapped his holstered gun on his hip. Then he ducked into his den and came out shoving something into his hip pocket. He looked big, mean and ugly, like he was all ready for a shoot-out. "Let's go," he said gruffly.

Chapter 4

MYSTERY OF THE MAN WHO WASN'T MISSING

Sheriff Landry told me to leave my bike at his house, where I could pick it up later. He got into his souped-up Pontiac, and I scrambled to get in the other side before he took off.

"Where's Minerva?" I asked.

"Funny you should ask. She's down at the library doing some research for a book report."

"She should have called me. I could have gone with her."

"Oh, no," Sheriff Landry said, picking up speed. "We need you around for reporting all these odd crimes. If we had you stuck away in the library, nothing would ever happen in this town."

"Very funny," I said. "I'll bet you'll be thanking me in a little while for being your first witness to the crime."

"Oh, brother," he said shaking his head. "I can see now why your old man spends so much time away from home fixing up old houses."

"Ho ho," I said, bracing my feet as he whipped into the next turn. "Wait and see. I'm nearly sorry I reported this crime before I found out how much the reward is."

He grinned, showing his long teeth. Wolflike, too, like the rest of him. "Don't count your money yet. So far all you've got is a report on a car coming out of a driveway."

He hit Steamboat Road then and put the Pontiac into overdrive. I expected the car to take off any second. There are times I've driven with Sheriff Landry and he points out the speed limit and all the stop signs, and how to wait for signals to change. This wasn't one of those times. When he's on an emergency call, he drives like a kamikaze pilot.

The big car roared to Tupelo Lane. He braked, spun the wheel hard, and zoomed down the long driveway. The tires grabbed in a jolting skidding stop, gravel bouncing off the car like hail.

"Let's go," he said. "You're the citizen making the complaint. If Mr. Waldorf is missing, abducted, kidnapped, or whatever, we'll start with your story and compare it with the servants'."

I followed him out.

Sheriff Landry rapped hard on the paneled Georgian door. It was flanked on either side by two bays. They were dimly lit but after his knock, another light went on. I could hear somebody inside walking toward the door.

The door opened and a man stood there looking inquiringly at us. I didn't like the way he was looking. He was staring right at Sheriff Landry's bronze police badge, and he showed no indication of grabbing the Sheriff's arm and yelling, "They went that way!"

"I'm Police Chief Landry," the Sheriff said. "Official business. I'd like a word with Mr. Gunther Waldorf, please."

The man nodded like a polite butler. He didn't say, "Ha ha, fat chance!" Instead he said, "One moment, please," and turned around to walk back inside.

Oh, boy, I told myself, wait till he finds out. That butler servant must really be goofing off on his job, I thought, not to have noticed that his employer wasn't around, having been kidnapped about an hour ago.

Sheriff Landry, I noticed, stood there unconcerned, as if he was used to important people being kidnapped, or else he still didn't put too much stock in my story. I knew he would be acting a lot more excited when the butler came running back in a panic.

The next moment things got spooky. The door opened wide. A thin, middle-aged, and white-haired man wearing wire-rimmed glasses stood there looking at us. I sucked in my breath.

"Mr. Waldorf? Gunther Waldorf?" Sheriff Landry asked.

The man nodded. "Yes?"

I couldn't do anything but stare.

"Sorry to trouble you," the Sheriff said. "But my daughter is doing a book report on ecology, taking in a study of the local environment. I was hoping you could recommend some of your books for her. Any particular title that you'd suggest?"

The man in the doorway looked pleased, and rumpled his white hair. "I'm sorry," he said shyly. "There are so many, I forget for the moment. Also I am so absentminded. Perhaps if you would call back later?"

Sheriff Landry smiled. "I've heard about you absent-minded professors." He reached into his hip pocket and produced an old paperback. He read off the title: *"The Population Peril.* We've got one of your older ones, fortunately. I suppose she could read this one meanwhile, and look up your others at the library. No need to trouble you again."

The man blinked. "Well—"

Sheriff Landry still smiling, took a pen from his pocket. "I'd appreciate it if you autographed this copy for my daughter. It would be a big thrill for her."

"A pleasure for me, too, if it helps," the man said. He took the pen and book from the Sheriff. "Her name?"

"Minerva Landry."

The man braced the book against the doorjamb. He wrote rapidly on the inside cover in big sprawling strokes. When he handed it back to the Sheriff, he smiled shyly again. "We don't get too many requests for our autograph, especially from the young people."

His accent was as I remembered it. European. Swiss or German.

Sheriff Landry was tucking the book back into his

pocket. "In that case, my kid will feel specially honored. Thanks a lot. Incidentally, I told your servant I was here on official business. I should have said personal."

The man half-bowed from the waist stiffly. "I can understand the concern of a policeman father. Is there anything else?"

He was looking at me now, as if expecting another book to autograph. I shook my head. "I'm with him," I said.

He said good night then, and stepped back smiling. The big door closed softly, and we walked back to the car. The house lights dimmed. The old pines behind sighed and swayed in the night wind.

Sheriff Landry drove around the circular drive and headed slowly down the long driveway. He stopped short of the sidewalk of Steamboat Road and looked back. "This about where you were when it happened? The two men dragging that leaning man into the waiting car back there?" He pointed up the drive.

"Right, Sheriff. I was crossing the driveway right here. The wind blew me to a stop."

"Check me if I'm wrong," he said. "I make it about fifty yards from here to the front of the house. Okay?"

I looked back with him and nodded. "Yeah. Okay."

"Happened between four and five o'clock?"

"I don't know exactly. Yeah, near there."

"Visibility was better then, I'll admit. But it's still a long way for anybody to pinpoint a face and be sure of an identity. Leaning at an angle, you also said, with two men dragging him. At this distance, could you be sure?"

"Yeah, Sheriff. Pretty sure, but—"

His cold voice cut in. "You saw a man who reminded you of Gunther Waldorf. Being dragged away, or hurried, or being helped. Could be any of those, right?"

I swallowed hard. I was used to the Sheriff always checking me out to make certain I knew my facts. He didn't buy anything but facts.

"Yes, sir," I said. "Any of those three covers it."

"But you did even better than that," he said. "You were right here, you said, when the speeding car came at you. Without lights, horn, or any warning, right? It narrowly missed hitting you, right? Then it hit the street, and you could look right into the car window and see Gunther Waldorf sitting on the rear seat between the two strangers. Closeup view, right?"

"Yes, sir. Just like you said."

He nodded and slowly eased his Pontiac out of the driveway and into the street. He checked both directions carefully for oncoming traffic, and then swung north and picked up speed. "All right, Steve. I think you got a fair shake back there. Any questions?"

I shook my head. "No, sir. His servant didn't act like he was missing. Gunther Waldorf was there. He autographed your book for Minerva. He didn't look guilty or surprised, or afraid of the law, or even grateful to see you for protection or any complaint. So I guess he wasn't kidnapped, after all."

"But you don't believe it, do you?"

"I know it's dumb, but yeah, I don't. How come he couldn't remember any of the books he wrote?"

The Sheriff shrugged. "It's a point, but he admitted

being absentminded. It's the old stereotype of professors, scientists, geniuses, and the like. They have too many things going on inside their heads to remember little things like normal people do."

"Maybe," I said. "If you take his word for it."

He shook his head and whistled through his teeth. "You've seen Mr. Waldorf before, you told me, when you were working your paper route?"

I nodded. "Not a lot, but enough times. He didn't always come to the door, but I've seen him working around the yard, trimming his trees, cleaning the flower beds, and so on. Even spoken to him. I got to admit this guy looks an awful lot like him."

"Spoke like him, too? Would you buy that?"

"Yes. The same kind of voice and accent. I think he spoke like him even more than he looked like him."

The Sheriff wrenched his wheel around the last turn leading east into the Point estates off Jonah's Bay, where he lived. His voice was sharper now, hotter. "Now what is that supposed to mean? Are you trying to tell me that man back there is an impostor—not Gunther Waldorf?"

His headlights picked up his driveway ahead, and the car ate up the remaining distance quickly. "I don't know what he is, Sheriff. Maybe if I hadn't seen the whole thing—seen the other man in the car—"

He spun the car into his driveway deftly and braked. He kept it idling with the lights on, and he looked straight ahead calmly. But his voice was getting rougher. "You never give up, do you? You're like your bulldog. Nothing stops you."

"Well, Sheriff, you asked me—"

He shook his head, growling now. "The man is right there, big as life, not a foot away from you. He looks like Waldorf, he sounds like Waldorf, he autographs a book as if he's Waldorf."

I thought fast. "Maybe when you check his autograph against his regular signature—"

He pounded the wheel with his big fist and cut me off. "You're still trying to tell me he's a phony, not the real ecologist. Why?"

"Well, if he's the real Gunther Waldorf, who was the guy they took away who looked so much like him?"

The Sheriff looked at me now witheringly. "I've only your word for that. You get a fast glimpse of a man there with two other men, and the car shoots toward you—all split-second timing—and you know it's Gunther Waldorf."

"Also he wasn't wearing an overcoat," I said.

He cut the engine then, and the lights, and got out of the car. I went out the other side. I got on my bike, ready to take off.

"What kind of car were they driving, Steve?" he said.

"Black Lincoln Continental. Late model. License plate NK 3163." I didn't realize I had remembered the plate. "New York State."

He jotted it down in a pad. "No overcoat, you said."

I shrugged. "Maybe he's a fresh-air fiend."

He took the folded poster circular I had given him out of his squall coat pocket, unfolded it, and read it over again. "If you're right, you know what I'm going to do?"

I shook my head, puzzled.

"I'll eat this poster," he said. He lifted his chin toward a nearby telephone pole. "Maybe part of that pole, too."

I noticed something white fluttering on the pole. I pedaled up to it. "It's another one," I called to the Sheriff. "Vote for Bradley Case." I reached up and tore it off tape and all. "You want it?"

His voice lashed at me. "Put it back. It's against the law to remove a public notice posted with intent to run for office here."

I put it back. I waited, but the Sheriff didn't say anything more. I waved good-bye and pedaled off. After a while I looked back. Sheriff Landry was still standing there looking at the poster on the pole telling everybody who could read that Bradley Case wanted his job.

I rode away fast before he remembered, and decided to nail me for removing the first one.

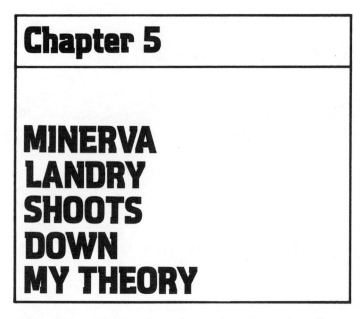

Chapter 5

MINERVA LANDRY SHOOTS DOWN MY THEORY

My mom was home from her job and starting dinner when I got back. She told me I had just missed a call from my dad. It seemed he would be delayed a few more days on the old Victorian he was remodeling for a customer out at Montauk. My old man is an artist and architect who works on old houses sometimes to make some extra bread in between doing his stuff on canvases. He's an expert on the old houses, and he gets calls from people who want the old authentic look so they have something to show for their money.

After dinner I went upstairs to my room with Sinbad to fill him in on the day's happenings. He was lying there in front of me with his head on his paws, paying close attention, when the phone rang. It was Minerva, Sheriff Landry's daughter. She's a year younger than me. One of those blue-eyed blondes you hear about who can get you in trouble.

Mrs. Landry died a long time ago, and he's never remarried. It's been just the Sheriff and Minerva ever since, with a housekeeper to do the house cleaning and make the meals. My old man and the Sheriff have been friends for a long time, and Minerva and I grew up together. She knows me like an old book, and isn't afraid to tear up the pages.

"I can't believe you are really for real," she said right off. "My pop said I should call you in case you might be talking to yourself. What's all this about you seeing Gunther Waldorf kidnapped from in front of his own house? Just because some guy forgot his overcoat?"

I told Sinbad who was calling. The love light came on in his brown eye, and his short tail thumped the floor. He's crazy about her.

"The man looked like him, Minerva," I told her. "So I figured I would report it to your old man because that's his job more than mine. I can't help it if this other guy happened to be back at the house later who looked like him."

"Maybe he has a twin brother. Did you ever think of that?"

I looked at Sinbad, and covered the mouthpiece. "She's got a good point on this kidnapping. A twin brother. I never thought of that." He listened, looking bored.

"Hello, you still there?" Minerva shouted.

"Yeah. I was just telling Sinbad what you said about the twin idea. He didn't think too much about it."

"Did you tell him your neat idea about the Citizens' Committee being behind the kidnapping?"

"Well, no, not yet."

"I can't wait till you tell him. I'll bet he'll be the first dog to tell the Board of Health his master has gone mad."

"It was just a theory, Minerva," I said. "It sort of went with the poster and the kidnapping, and all."

"The trouble with you," she said, "is that you always shoot your mouth off before you know what you're talking about. According to what you told my pop, we don't have a dirty county that needs cleaning up, right?"

"Right, and just because they say so—"

"Listen, dumbbell," she said interrupting me, "would you take the word of an expert on it?"

"I guess so. Only who—?"

"How does the name of Gunther Waldorf grab you? I was reading some of his books before at the library."

"Gunther Waldorf said our county of Hampton was dirty and needed cleaning up?"

"You better believe it," she said. "In his book *The Poison Around Us*—he says the bay is polluted, the air is polluted, the oyster beds are polluted, and our drinking water is polluted."

"When did he say all this?" I asked nervously.

"It's not just in that one book, it's in all of them. Since he got here, ten years ago, that's all he's been writing about. How rotten things are getting to be in Hampton, compared to how they were in the good old days."

"Well, how come nobody's done anything about it?"

"I guess because nobody's died of the plague yet," she said. "So people don't pay much attention to him."

"Then maybe that's why the Citizens' Committee had him kidnapped," I said excitedly. "So he'll work for them and tell them exactly what's wrong and how to go about fixing everything up. You know, like with those atomic bomb scientists they kidnap, to make them tell how it works, or else."

She laughed shrilly. "Oh, brother, I think I'd better hang up before we both go crazy. I'll check with you tomorrow at school. If you're not there, I'll know they put you away."

Sinbad cocked his head at the click. "She hung up," I told him. "She didn't think too much about my last theory, either."

I called another conference. Starting again with the poster, then the car in the driveway. Sinbad stared without blinking, but then his eyes started to close.

"Stay awake," I told him. "Now I'm coming to the real clue—the important part about the missing overcoat."

There was a low buzzing sound. Sinbad was snoring.

"Okay. The meeting will be continued after you wake up. Don't forget where we were." I went down to help Mom with the dishes. When I got back to my room Sinbad was fast asleep in my bed. We always have slept together. He opened one eye when I got into bed. "Tomorrow's another day," I told him. "Maybe we'll get a break and tear this case wide open for the Sheriff."

Sinbad let his eye close again. It was okay with him.

Chapter 6

BIG PUNCH-OUT AT SCHOOL

The next morning, as I rode past Mrs. Teska's store on my way to school, I noticed she still had the blue card in her window that said CLOSED. She usually has the store open at that time. I made up my mind to check later after school to find out what was going on with her.

Minerva Landry found me at school. She's always in high spirits and not afraid to speak her mind. I think she would be that way even if she wasn't the Sheriff's daughter. She greeted me by punching me on the arm, as usual. "I didn't hear anything on the radio or TV about anybody being kidnapped or missing," she said, right off. "There wasn't anything in the newspaper this morning, either. I think you must have dreamed up that Gunther Waldorf kidnapping incident."

"That's what your old man thinks, Minerva. But I wasn't dreaming. I was right there when it happened."

"When what happened?" she said. "If he was there in the house when you and my pop went back there, he couldn't be kidnapped or missing, could he? If you ask me, I think it's your brain that's missing."

"Maybe they got scared when they noticed I happened to be there as a witness, and brought him right back," I said.

"Was Sinbad there with you at the time?" I shook my head negative. "Well, then your last guess is wrong, too. Without Sinbad you couldn't scare anybody."

"Maybe they just took him back to their hideout, and pumped some drug into him so he would forget what happened. Asked him some questions and then hypnotized him, you know. I've seen that in a lot of TV movies."

She punched my other arm. "In less than an hour? It takes longer than that for a drug to work, dumbbell, and sometimes even longer for a person to be hypnotized."

"Maybe they're getting better at it," I said. "So they could speed it all up and do it faster."

"I think somebody speeded up your brain once and now it's all shot. If they have him all drugged and hypnotized, why would they bring him back? And about those pollution questions, if they want to know something, all they have to do is read his books."

"That's another strange thing, about his books. This fellow saying he was Gunther Waldorf couldn't remember any of the titles of his books. Isn't that weird?"

"Not if he's busy working on another one, dummy, and his mind is tuned out to everything else that happened. If you'd have written as many books as he has, all on the same subject, I bet you wouldn't remember one from the other, either."

"Well, maybe," I said. "But I remember everything I saw yesterday evening, and it's all still up here"—I tapped my head—"just the way it happened."

"If it's still up there where you pointed, it's stuck in a lot of fat that you have between your ears. Maybe you ought to try a riddle and get your brain used to thinking again. What's soft and yellow and goes plop plop plop?"

Minerva always stumps me with her riddles. I gave it a quick thought. "Sorry, I can't—"

"A leaky banana. Why do hippos stay in the river all the time?"

I shook my head. "Nope. I got to give up on that too."

"Because they're afraid to step on butterflies." She looked at her watch. "I got to go to the school library now. What new dumb thing are you going to do next, so I don't have to wait until it happens, and can start laughing now?"

"Maybe I'm not the only dumb one around. You ought to be out tearing off all those posters with Bradley Case running for sheriff. Did you see them yet?"

"Well, yeah, there's one right in front of our house."

"And you left it hanging up there? Don't you realize this guy Case might knock your old man out of office?"

Minerva hooted. "Are you for real? He's been sheriff

of this town before you or I were born. The people here always vote my pop back into office."

"I know that. So far, anyway. But neither you nor your old man seem to understand that a bunch of new people have moved into town the last few years. And a lot of the old Landry voters have moved away. So what's to stop the new ones from getting together and deciding it's time to put one of their own guys in?"

She thought about it. "You think they can?"

"Why not? All it takes is enough of them to vote for this Bradley Case, and he's got your pop's job."

Her blue eyes looked thoughtful. "I hate to agree with you, but this time maybe you have a point."

"If you want to, I'll help you take down a lot of those posters. What they don't see won't hurt. Only don't tell your old man it was my idea."

She looked happy. "Maybe you're not so weird, after all. I'll let you know. See you later."

She punched me in the arm and ran down the hall. If we ever get married, I know one of the first things we'll have to talk about is this arm-punching business.

Chapter 7

THE TROUBLE WITH MRS. TESKA

After school I took Sinbad out for his afternoon walk. The white card that spelled OPEN was in Mrs. Teska's store window, and I didn't have to ask Sinbad twice about paying the old lady a visit.

She was sitting in her chair near the potbellied stove. Compared to outside, the store was warm, but Mrs. Teska was wearing her thick red wool shawl. Sinbad whined and nearly yanked my arm off trying to get to her. She patted him and rubbed his ears, telling him how glad she was to see him. Sinbad wagged his tail happily and stood there drooling, his big dark head against her knee.

"How you, Stevie?" she said. "It pretty cold outside, no?"

"Yeah," I said. "I thought you were sick or something. How come you had your store closed?"

She shrugged her thick shoulders. "Oh, this old lady have to go see somebody. Some kind of business."

"Also, while I'm here, I better remind you election is coming up soon, Mrs. Teska. Sheriff Landry is running for office again. You won't forget to vote, will you?"

"Maybe so, Stevie, if still here."

"Why, where you going, Mrs. Teska?" I said. "Some kind of trip?"

She smiled. "Maybe so, Stevie. Special trip where old peoples go." She raised her head and looked toward the store ceiling. "Maybe pretty soon, Mrs. Teska go, too."

I looked at her. She seemed to be okay. Tan from all her outdoor gardening work, only a few fine wrinkles showing on her face. "That's no way to talk, Mrs. Teska. You're not sick or anything, are you?"

She shook her head. "No sick, no. Mrs. Teska never sick. You know that, Stevie." She rapped her knuckles on the wooden armchair. "Always is good health. Maybe sometimes is tired, but never sick, no."

"So what are you talking about? You might live another ten or twenty years yet."

She sighed heavily. "No way to know, Stevie. Anyway, is good to be ready. My sister Sofi she be telling me it not be so bad."

"I didn't know you had a sister. Where does she live?"

"Sofi no live now, Stevie. She young sister of Mrs. Teska. Die a long time ago when very young back in old country."

"I don't get it, Mrs. Teska," I said. "What do you mean, she's been telling you—?"

She looked at me suspiciously. "You not get mad if Mrs. Teska tell you?"

I laughed. "Are you kidding? Why would I get mad at you?"

She shrugged again, sat back, and rubbed her face. Her voice sounded tight, hoarser. "Sofi is talk to me lately, Stevie. She is tell me all about for to be ready. That it not be so bad for to die."

"You mean, you've been dreaming about her—your sister Sofi?"

She shook her head. "No, no. Is no dream. Is real. I hear her voice. Sofi talk to me. I remember how she sound. So it be her, all right."

"I don't get it," I said, puzzled. "How does she do that?"

She smiled. "Mrs. Teska hear about this man. He like holy man, is very nice. He speak with spirits. Spirits only talk for good man, you know, Stevie. So when Mrs. Teska come to his house, he get Sofi's spirit to talk to me."

"You mean, he's some kind of psychic? I didn't know we had any in our town."

She nodded. "His name Solo Yerkos. Him very fine person, help this old lady. If not for him, maybe I die and not settle affairs in time."

"What does that mean?" I said.

She threw her hands outward. "It mean, if Mrs. Teska be to die, what good is for to own store and business? No can take along when die. So Sofi give me good advice. She know all about what dead spirit need. Is nothing to take."

It was Mrs. Teska's money, and none of my affair. But although she lived simply and ran a small general food and grocery store on Steamboat Road on the low-income side of town, she wasn't any kind of poor old lady.

Not by a couple of million dollars!

I remembered her story. That a long time ago, when she was a young girl new to this country, and very beautiful, she had been married to a notorious gambler, Big Nick Murdock. Then, as a result of being linked to a crime he had never committed, he was forced to live abroad.

He came back many years later, when it was established that he was innocent. By this time both he and Mrs. Teska were old. Because I was able to solve the mystery which cleared him, I became friends with his lawyer, Mr. Gideon Pickering. And he got Big Nick Murdock and Mrs. Teska together again. Big Nick fondly remembered his old romance with Mrs. Teska, and promised he was going to take care of her for the years ahead, although they had been divorced for a long time. I felt that because Big Nick Murdock was still rich and a very generous man, he would take care of Mrs. Teska in the only way he knew. Kingstyle. He wasn't the type to go back on his word.

I didn't know for sure what he had left her, but I could guess it was plenty. It was possible that Mrs. Teska didn't even know her financial situation. And so I smelled something fishy going on here. "What does your sister tell you to do with your money, Mrs. Teska?"

She shrugged. "She say is no good for to keep. Is better to give away, Sofi say."

"Well, I mean, who are you supposed to give it to—charity?"

She shook her head. "Is not decided yet, Stevie. Maybe next time, Sofi will say. She say to be ready meanwhile. And when Mrs. Teska go to this Solo Yerkos man again, maybe she say then, and I know. You see, is good thing for to do, yes?"

"Gee, I don't know, Mrs. Teska," I said. "I mean, you ought to think about it. But she's your own sister. I guess she knows what's good for you."

She nodded, seeming pleased that I agreed with her. When we left, something was bothering me but I didn't know exactly what until we were nearly home. Sinbad was sniffing along, head down, chasing every fresh scent, towing me along down our hill so fast that I had to run to keep up with him.

Sinbad sneezed and I said, "Gesundheit!" And suddenly I thought about Sofi, Mrs. Teska's sister. In all the years I'd known Mrs. Teska, practically since I was born, I'd never heard her mention having a sister. It seemed strange for her to be suddenly talking about one now.

We were in front of our house now, and I leaned back and yanked on the leash. "Time to go inside," I told him. He scowled up at me. "Make a note," I told him. "How do we know for sure that Mrs. Teska's sister Sofi is for real? I mean, what if this guy Solo Yerkos is some kind of a crook, and he's out to get Mrs. Teska's money?"

Ordinarily, Sinbad would have thought about it, and given me a sign. But this time he was too disappointed that he had to leave all those mysterious scents blowing around, and go inside.

He just looked up at me, kind of disgusted.

"Well, think about it anyway," I told him. "I've got a real hunch about this one."

Chapter 8

TELLING
IT
LIKE
IT IS

Minerva Landry dropped over. She was wearing a thin squall coat over a red checked shirt. Her long blond hair looked as if it had lost a fight to the wind. She was holding something white rolled up in her hand. She opened it to show me the Bradley Case poster for sheriff put out by that Citizens' Committee for a Cleaner County.

"Well, that's one less out there staring people in the face," she said. "I took your word for it that this guy could use less advertising."

"Too bad your old man doesn't feel the same way, Minerva. I forgot to tell you that he told me when I ripped one off it was against the law to remove a posted notice of somebody running for public office. He'll probably ground you when he finds out."

She shrugged and started banging Sinbad around. "That's a crazy law. Besides, this thing was hanging right outside our house on the nearest pole. I couldn't stand looking at the dumb thing."

"If it was my old man running for reelection, I'd go around taking all of them down. Honest. Besides, this guy Case is a crook."

Sinbad had rolled over on his back. Minerva was swatting him hard. He was making a lot of fake growls pretending this was a great wrestling match they were having. Meanwhile his stubby tail was wagging like crazy. He really digs Minerva.

She looked back at me. "Do you happen to know that for a fact, or is this another of your weird theories—like the way they kidnapped the wrong Gunther Waldorf?"

I picked up the poster. "Take a look for yourself. Look how close together his eyes are. You can tell he's a crook, just like that whole Citizens' Committee is. If they win the election, wait and see. Remember I predicted it first."

Minerva let go of Sinbad and studied the picture. "Lots of people's eyes are close together, dumbbell. That doesn't prove anything."

"Name one I know," I said.

She laughed. "Well, I hate to say this but have you looked in your mirror lately?"

"Ho ho," I said. I didn't want to give Minerva the satisfaction of seeing me jump up and run to a mirror, although I knew I'd be checking on that after she left.

"But don't take it to heart," she said. "I happen to know you're honest. So that takes care of that theory.

Now how do you know this committee is crooked? Do you have any evidence? I mean, have you seen any canceled checks to show they've bought out somebody, or like that?"

"Not yet," I said. "I haven't had time to get into that yet. But you can see they've got these posters all over town. That shows how anxious they are to snow the people and get all the votes they can. And once they get in—whammo! They'll make this town wish it had never been born. Watch and see."

She shook her head. "I can see now why you always drive my old man nuts. You use your imagination instead of facts. These posters are cheaper to get out than advertising on TV. They put them all over so the voters get an idea of who's running for office. What's wrong with that? If my pop's campaign party ever gets going, they'll be doing the same thing. I wish just one time, for the sake of novelty, you would tell me one thing you happen to know is true."

"Well," I said, a little annoyed, "Mrs. Teska is getting ready to die. Now that's a true fact because she told me so herself only a little while ago."

Minerva looked surprised. "She told you that?"

"But first she's going to give her money away."

"How come?"

"Because her sister Sofi told her to."

"I didn't know Mrs. Teska had a sister."

"She doesn't," I said. Minerva's eyes narrowed and I knew her next move would be to punch my arm, so I moved back a little. "The sister died long ago she said, when they were both living in the old country—Serbia, or wherever it was."

But Minerva looked thoughtful instead. "Her dead sister talking to her? Isn't that weird?"

I nodded. "She's been going to some kind of medium, she told me. He puts her in touch with her sister's spirit, she says."

"And she believes him? Wow, that's terrific. Is he for real? What's his name?"

"Solo Yerkos. Well, she says he's for real, but I got my doubts."

Minerva smiled. "Right on. You're probably thinking he's a crook, too, right? You've got crooks on the brain."

"Well, it won't hurt to find out something about him," I said. "Just in case. I don't like that part about her sister telling her to get rid of her money. Why does she have to do that?"

"Well, Mrs. Teska is very old, isn't she?"

"Over seventy, I guess. So what?"

"So, let's say that she feels she hasn't too much longer to live, even without the medium or her sister telling her anything. So then what's wrong with giving her money away first? She can't do it afterward, can she?"

"No, but—"

"Well, wait," Minerva said, "there is one way. She can write her will, I guess. Then that takes care of anything she wants done after she dies."

I wished I'd thought about the will. One of the

good things about Minerva is her thinking. Her brain is faster and clearer, when it counts, than mine.

"She didn't mention that. I better talk to her about it. Maybe I can talk her into seeing her lawyer before she does anything."

"I don't see why you have to butt in at all," Minerva said. "She's always been a smart old lady. What makes you think she suddenly forgot how to think straight? For all you know, this guy Solo Yerkos might be doing her a big favor by putting her in touch with her dead sister's spirit. Then when she passes over, she'll have somebody near her. Maybe her sister will guide her to the rest of her passed-over family."

"She didn't mention that," I said slowly.

"Maybe spirits don't have that much time to talk about everything," Minerva said. "For all you know, Mrs. Teska has a whole lot of dead relatives—maybe brothers, cousins, aunts, uncles, and so on. People from the old country always had a whole lot of relatives, I think. Real big families. And somebody was always dying."

"She didn't mention that, either," I said. "But I don't see what's so terrible about telling her to see her lawyer first."

Minerva punched her open hand. "Well, you know how lawyers work. They'll want some proof to protect her. So they'll ask this Solo Yerbos a lot of questions about how he's getting her sister to talk to her. And then they'll start asking her sister to prove she's really her sister—"

"What's wrong with that?" I interrupted.

"—and by that time," Minerva continued, "her sister might say 'who needs this hassle?' and drop back to the spirit world. Then they'll put the medium out of business, or throw him in the pokey. And by the time Mrs. Teska dies, she won't have anybody to lead her around up there, and might become one of those lost souls you hear about."

"That spirit jazz sounds like a big fake to me," I said. "Do you really think that could happen?"

Minerva shrugged. "How do I know? How do I know what happens up there? It's possible, I guess. But the lawyer might ruin everything. And I know you better than the lawyer, so I'm betting on you to do it."

I could see where maybe Minerva had a point. "Maybe you're right. I'll let her alone and mind my own business."

Minerva's blue eyes sparkled. "Wanna bet?"

I guess she knows me better than I do. After she left, I remembered to check my eyes. They weren't that close together.

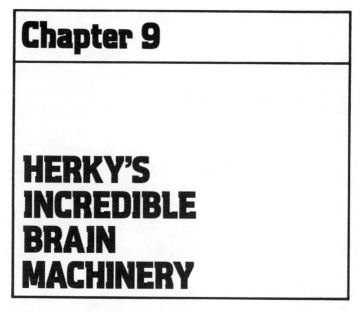

Chapter 9

HERKY'S INCREDIBLE BRAIN MACHINERY

After Minerva Landry buzzed off, I told Sinbad we better have a conference real fast. I got down on the floor with him, and he settled into his flying-squirrel position, flat down with his head on his paws. Not moving a muscle but just looking steadily at me with that love light gleaming in his eyes.

"Okay, you heard it all before and how Minerva thinks I'm dreaming again. So the purpose of this meeting is to see if she's right or I am. You be the judge."

Sinbad's tail thumped rapidly on the floor a few times, and then gradually slowed to a final thump. He was letting me know he was paying attention.

"Right off we got three mysteries," I told him. "We got Gunther Waldorf being kidnapped even though he's still there, or seems to be. We got Mrs. Teska, who is very healthy, getting ready to die and give away her money because her dead sister Sofi is telling her to. And we got Sheriff Landry not doing anything at all about his reelection campaign while this creep Bradley Case has his picture plastered all over town by that phony Citizens' Committee for a Cleaner County."

Sinbad sighed softly and closed one eye. Sometimes that meant he understood, and sometimes it meant I'd better talk fast before he fell asleep.

"Stay awake," I told him. "All we got to do is decide which one we tackle first. I figure the top two are the most important. Do you agree?"

There was the sound of snoring. Both eyes were nearly closed.

"So I've decided to let Herky in on it. Okay?"

Sinbad thumped his little tail feebly, closed both eyes, let out a long blubbering sigh, and fell asleep.

"Okay," I said. "Just as long as we both agree."

I left him lying there in dreamland, and got on my squall coat for the long bike ride to Herky Krakower's house. I could have called him and got the information over the phone, but Herky was crippled when he was a little kid, and doesn't get out too much, so I knew he would appreciate the visit.

Herky didn't have too much strength in his arms or legs, so what he did was develop his brain instead. He had become a human computer who never forgot anything he had ever read. He was a mathematical wizard, a superbrain in science, and had operated at the college level since he was eleven. I liked Herky because he was the only genius I knew, and he liked me because he lived to accumulate knowledge. I was an expert on old houses, what went into them, what made them special and different, so we had our own mutual admiration society.

It was a cold ride to the middle of the village, where Herky lived with his mother. She teaches retarded children at a special school. Always nice, a cool lady, she invited me inside without making any big deal about using the mat outside the door to wipe my feet.

"You've been away too long," she said. "He gets more out of one adventure with you than from a dozen library books."

"Well, this isn't really an adventure, Mrs. Krakower. Not yet, anyway. I just came over to pump Herky's brain a little. It's only a little problem."

She laughed. "As I recall, those little ones become bigger once you and Herky get together. By the time you're finished, we'll have the FBI all over town."

Herky's upstairs room was like the lab of a sci-fi mad scientist. Books overflowed the wall shelves onto the floor. A telescope was mounted on a tripod near the windows. On the other side of the room, counters and tables were cluttered with glass beakers and chemicals. Since he's a rock hound and interested in mineralogy, he had a collection of assorted rocks, too. Papers and magazines covered his desk. Scraps of paper with scribbled notations, charts, and graphs were pinned on the wall.

In one corner were miniature clay and plaster models of streamlined automobiles of the future, spaceships, models of housing. And finally my eyes rested on a wonderfully contrived model of city streets, stacked on different levels, that moved on slowly revolving cogwheels.

"What's that?" I asked.

Herky grinned shyly. "An experiment in saving energy. I'm moving the streets instead of the cars. They drive onto certain levels, and are turned and funneled off to their destination without having to use gas driving there."

I bent closer to look at it. "What's it called?"

"Chaos," he said.

I pointed to a large cogwheel interlocked with a smaller one moving like clockwork. "But doesn't that use a lot of energy?"

"No, it's powered by solar and geothermal energy. The heat and magnetic power of the earth. Thermodynamics. If you want the details—" He reached for a thick stack of notes on his desk.

I shook my head. "No, thanks, I'd never understand it. If you say it works, I'll take your word for it, Herky."

He leaned toward one of the slowly spinning wheels topped with small models of cars and trucks. "There's only one problem with it."

"Like what?" It looked too good to have any flaws.

He pointed to a line of toy cars being moved off at a cloverleaf intersection. "If somebody isn't quite sure where he's going, and I have him dropped off here, he can't get right back on. He'll have to go through the entire moving process again."

"That's okay, Herk. Next time he'll know where he's going."

Herky smiled. "Either that, or they shoot the inventor."

Watching how Herky figured out how to move a traffic-congested city around made me feel foolish about troubling him with my problem. Herky's head was always in the stars, and I would be bringing him back down to earth. But, as usual, he made it easier for me.

"Now let's talk about something important," he said, sitting back in his chair. "What's happening with you?"

I filled him in from the beginning: the new election posters, the questionable kidnapping, and finally Mrs. Teska's strange story.

Herky rubbed his hands. "That's it? I counted three."

"I decided to let you in at the beginning, Herk. I'm not making headway with any of them."

He shrugged. "It would be nice if they were related. That would make it an interesting puzzle. Do you think they are?"

"Only the election posters and the Waldorf kidnapping. But I can't prove anything, Herk."

"Well, let's consider them in sequence. The election posters in themselves mean nothing. Part of our democratic process. On the alleged Gunther Waldorf kidnapping, while I don't question what you saw, I'm sure Sheriff Landry must have covered all possible angles with you already, and he's a competent lawman. If he's convinced the man there is Waldorf, you'll have to accept that as fact, Steve."

"That's one of the problems, Herk. I can't. Even though it seems to be a fact."

He nodded. "Unless you uncover evidence to the contrary, and especially that which would make the kidnapping part of a criminal plot of the Citizens' Committee. Do you plan to dig into their activities?"

"You bet," I said. "But what's happening with Mrs. Teska bothers me the most. I've known her since I was a little kid, and I hate to hear her talking about dying now—especially when she seems in good health. Not to mention giving away everything she owns."

Herky looked thoughtful, and was scribbling notes to himself. "That seems to be a two-part problem. The first part is psychological, dealing with and depending upon Mrs. Teska's emotional condition. Her age is a factor. Older people, I understand, tend to begin planning for their approaching death, as they advance in years. Some welcome it, others fear it. Apparently Mrs. Teska is in the process of getting herself organized, as a person used to taking care of herself, with no dependents, nobody to look after her."

"Okay, I understand that, but I can't depend on her deciding what's best for her. I can't guess what's in her mind. And she's taking this medium's word for everything. How do I know he's telling her the truth, not ripping her off?"

"You don't," Herky said, "and that's because of the second part of the problem—the psychic or medium Yerkos. Having her sister talk to her is one thing. That's the realm of the medium. But Mrs. Teska in deciding to hurry things up and die to join her sister is another.

It could be her own idea, or perhaps he is exercising some sort of mind control. Hypnosis, any form of suggestion like that.

"The disposal of her property can be managed properly. As a safeguard, she could have a will drawn up, which of course goes into effect only in the event of her death, making that giveaway money conditional."

"Minerva Landry thought of that, too," I said. "But what about this Yerkos guy? What if he's faking all that stuff about her sister and her spirit, putting her on? Do you believe that story about her sister's spirit coming back from the dead after all this time to talk to her?"

Herky's face, usually pale, was developing more color as he got into the problem. His dark eyes were glowing. "Believing is something else, Steve. I really don't know too much about the psychic world, you know."

Whenever Herky says he doesn't know much about something, I disregard it. He never lets on what he knows, and you have to dig it out of him. "Okay," I said. "Maybe you read something about it sometime."

He half-turned, gesturing to a stack of books behind him. "Oh, sure, I've read about cases, but I don't know anything from my own experience. That has to be taken into consideration." He nodded toward his transportation model. "It's like this gizmo working fine here in my room. But it's a different matter to make it work on real streets with real people in real cars and trucks, in a real-life situation. It's fine, theoretically, but—"

"Okay, Herk, what's your theory about how psychics and mediums work?"

"That comes under the third ESP, sometimes called PSI, category, having to do with survival phenomena—"

"Hold it, Herk. You're on the third already. What happened to the first two?"

He laughed. "Well, they're all part of the phenomenon called ESP, that is, extrasensory perception—an altered state of consciousness—but you asked me about psychics and mediums. The others are things like telepathy, clairvoyance, precognition, materialization, levitation—"

I held up my hand. "It's terrific how you don't know anything about it. Okay, tell me about the third one."

"It concerns events caused by discarnate personalities or entities. It includes mediumship, the ability to perceive or communicate with discarnates or to act as a channel through which discarnates communicate."

"Mrs. Teska's sister Sofi is a discarnate?"

He nodded. "There are a few more, all part of the same package, you might as well hear about."

"Okay. I'm sure glad I didn't ask you about something you knew about."

He grinned. "I'm wise to you, Steve. You only pretend to be dumb so you don't have to dig up all this information the same way I did, by reading all the stuff about it. Anyway, the next thing is spirit possession, which is directly related to your problem."

"About time. Let's hear it."

"It's a state known as possession, in which a person

seems to be under the control in mind and body of another personality, generally thought to be a discarnate, sometimes a nonhuman spirit."

I shook my head. "They've got those kind, too?"

"Remember, I've never experienced them—only read of it."

"Well, whoever wrote about it must have—unless they're making it all up."

Herky smiled. "I doubt that. There's too much evidence of psychic phenomena already. Where've you been?"

"Maybe I'll catch up with it all now, without having to read about it. So this psychic Solo Yerkos is acting as a channel for Mrs. Teska's sister's spirit—the discarnate Sofi?"

"Right. Unless he's putting her on, fooling her, as you seem to suspect, for his own ulterior motives."

I nodded quickly. "Yeah, that's how I feel. She's a superstitious old lady. I know from a lot of talks with her. She would go for something like this easily. This psychic could be on the level, an honest medium, but until I meet him and get to know more about him, I figure he's a rat fink."

Herky leaned back, checking his notes. "If he's a fraud, you could get Sheriff Landry to run a check on him. There's a special bunco department for that down at the D.A.'s office. But unless you can prove otherwise, Yerkos is presumed to be acting in good faith."

I got up. "Okay, maybe I can do that."

Herky lifted a warning finger. "How?"

"I don't know yet. There's something too fishy about

her sister's spirit coming along now, suddenly trying to get in touch with her—not long after this
guy Yerkos moves into our town. What took Sofi so
long?"

Herky shrugged. "Perhaps Yerkos provided the right
time and channel for her to appear—remember, he's
the medium—"

"Yeah, according to him, he is."

"Well, we don't know yet, do we, if he's a fake or
not? But there's something else you might want to
know, Steve—sometimes ghosts, or spirits, or appari-
tions, whatever you want to call them, come back because they're lost. It's as if they need to make contact
with somebody they once knew. Or it could be somebody they feel can help them."

"I don't get it," I said. "How can you help a ghost?"

"It depends," he said. "What you have there is a
restless spirit. From what I've read, it's as if they're
going around for a long time, like they're in a spell,
and they need somebody to contact to get them out
of it. So, getting back to Mrs. Teska, if she really believes it's her sister, naturally she'll do anything she
can. In a similar situation, you'd be inclined to do the
same thing."

"Maybe," I said. "But I'd have to see that to believe
it."

He gestured toward his bookshelf. "Care to borrow
some of these books to read up on it?"

"No, thanks, Herk. I'm sure you didn't leave out
anything."

"Well, if I can help—"

"Thanks again, but I still don't know what to do about anything."

He looked wistful when I left, as if he was being left out of something. I didn't have the heart to tell Herky that somebody with his intelligence shouldn't take ghosts and spirits that seriously.

Chapter 10

MYSTERY OF THE GHOST IN MY BEDROOM

Ever since I got him as a small pup, Sinbad and I have slept together. During the night we take turns using each other as a pillow. It happened to be his turn this night to be sleeping with his big head on my chest. Suddenly he jerked up, hitting my chin with his hard head, waking me up.

"Come on, cut it out, you big ape," I grumbled sleepily, reaching out to set him back in place. But Sinbad wasn't ready to go back to sleep. He was standing in front of me, facing the foot of the bed, his short ears perked up, whining softly. He whipped his head back to face me, looking worried, and when I saw what was over there, I didn't blame him.

It was a ghost, a pirate ghost, at least it looked like one, and for a long moment I held my breath, feeling a chill run up my back. Oh, no, I said to myself, this can't be happening. I'm seeing things. Maybe I'm dreaming. All that talking with Herky about spirits blew my mind.

Sinbad backed up to me, whining, and I held on to his strong thick neck, feeling him trembling with excitement, and then I knew there was no mistake. Sinbad was seeing the ghost, too.

I had a quick thought of running to the phone and calling Herky. "Herky," I would say, "you wanted to see a ghost or spirit so badly, well, come on over. I've got a real one here."

But, of course, I didn't. When you have a ghost in your bedroom around midnight, you don't fool around. You don't do anything but wait until the ghost tells you what he's doing there. What you are, really, is his prisoner for that period of time. All you can do is try not to swallow your heart or you count your goose bumps. Even with Sinbad there as my protector, I didn't feel much like kidding around.

"Avast!" the ghost said. "So you're the one responsible."

The first word was a nautical term, one you don't hear anymore, establishing him as a former seafaring man, and suiting his pirate outfit. But the last word had more meaning for me. It meant this ghostly visit wasn't any accident!

I wasn't sleepy now, and somehow not as frightened. I guess my curiosity won over. "Excuse me, sir," I said hesitantly, "responsible for what?"

His image swayed before me, flickering and unsteady, transparent, too—I could see right through him. He wore wide-flared white pants, torn and dirty, cut short above the ankles, a sleeveless shirt, and a red-stained, dirty bandage covered his right eye. No pirate boots. He was barefoot. His hair and beard were rough, long, and matted. Red, also, I thought. A long knife was tucked into the wide belt on his hip. He was chesty, husky, and appeared to be in his forties.

"There's been talk of ghosts and spirits," he said. "Got me ectoplasm all stirred up, ye might say." He leaned closer as if to inspect me with his visible cold blue eye. "Aye, ye have the looks of a lively lad, and I see ye have the breed I always been partial to—that's a seaman's dog, y'know, laddie. The likes of him rode the quarterdeck with yours truly, many's the time." He sighed and the intense cold he was projecting came across the room like a chilling wind. "An' now, it's the nature of the business I'm here for that we'll be discussin'."

"Business?" I said, figuring he had made a mistake, after all.

"Aye, lad. I want my share of the gold. I'll not be cheated of me own proper share."

"Yes, sir," I said. "Your share. Of the gold, you said."

His eye narrowed, squinting. "It was booty off the Spanish ship, the *Pricaro*. We plundered her proper, we did, matie, and scuttled her off the island there."

I cleared my throat. "What island was that, sir?"

He jerked his thumb toward the window. "The big one out there, lad. Looks like the head of a ram."

I sat up straighter. Twenty miles north across Jonah's Bay is an island called Ram's Head. "Ram's Head," I said. "Yeah, it's way out the Point."

He shook his head slowly, as if with an effort. "Don't misunderstand me now, mate. The gold's not there. They buried it ashore here. There was to be equal shares for the crew, but the bloody blackguards crossed John Francis Marion, they did, murdered him on the spot to guard the treasure, leavin' me to walk the bloody beach nigh two hundred years."

"Gee," I said, "I'm sorry about that, Mr. Marion."

His jaws separated in a gaping ghostly grin. "That'd be Captain Marion, if y'please. Although them what knowed me well called me Redbeard. But I'm mighty relieved to know that now ye'll be helpin' me."

"Well, sure, if I can," I said. "Only what good will the gold do you now? I mean, you said yourself you're dead—"

The ghost appeared to draw back. His form faded to a dim outline, like the flickering of a candle before its flame dies out. It was eerie watching his disappearing, but after the momentary dimming, he became brighter again, strongly visible. He took a deep, sighing, rasping breath. "It's the energy, lad." His hollow voice was fainter. "It's been so long since I made an appearance, I forget how to ration it."

"Well, if you're not feeling so hot, Captain Marion, we can make it some other time," I said.

His form glowed on and off, pulsating. "Aye, lad, we might have to do that. Meanwhile, you start looking around. East of Scuttle Point, off Jonah Bay, fathoms deep they dug it."

I shook my head at him hoping he would understand. "That's private property there, belonging to the Murdock estate. From Captain Billy Murdock. He was an old pirate himself. But his heirs own it, and I'd be arrested if I started digging. Besides that beach is a couple of miles long. Even if I started tomorrow, it could take me the rest of my life to find it for you."

He shook his fist impatiently. "It's buried in the cave, laddie. Now yer not tellin' me caves is private property?"

"They are if they're part of the Murdock land," I said.

He leaned back, swaying. "There's another thing. The cave where it was buried ain't the same no more. The hills came down since, an' there's no way of tellin' ye where."

"It's covered over now, you mean? Well, yeah, that makes it even tougher. But what I still don't understand is why you still have to hang around here for so many years. I thought ghosts could go anyplace."

His laugh was mournful and hollow. "Only up to a point, mate. An' one thing for sure is they can't cross water. Like as no spirit can. An' there's yer reason. So I been walkin' me beat, ye might say, these many years, guardin' the same bloomin' treasure I was cheated out of."

"Well, I'm sorry if I got you out of your rest periods. You said you haven't made any appearances lately."

He nodded. "Aye, lad. There's been times I clean forgot what I was still hangin' around for. The energy gets low and there's no reason to be movin' about. But somethin's been happenin' of late, somethin' goin' on out there, I can feel it in me bones. I know it's somethin' to do with me gold, and it's why I came direct to you."

Puzzled, I shook my head. "I still don't get the connection. I was only talking to a friend of mine about spirits. We weren't after your treasure."

"Aye, lad, I'm not disputin' what yer telling me. But back there over the beach where I do me rounds some nights, is where the vibration comes from now. Just startin' up, ye might say. It got me worried, and then to thinkin'. Now I can't rightly say why I came to you. There ain't no logic in bein' a shade, to start with, but the vibrations set me off, y'see, and I came straight here, so there's no mistake about it, for reasons unknown, I'm askin' yer help. There's a good lad."

"Well, okay," I said. "I don't know how to get started on this yet, but maybe some time if I meet you out there, you can give me better directions, to help you find it."

He laughed then, a strange high laugh. "Aye, lad, and when we do, I'll tell ye better why a dead man wants his share of the gold."

"Okay, sure," I said.

His form flared and then diminished. He moaned softly. "The spirit's leavin' me now, lad. I'll be back."

The window curtains I had glimpsed faintly through the ghost suddenly appeared clearer. I looked around. He was gone. The moon was shining brightly in a clear cloudless sky.

Sinbad whined, still staring straight ahead where the ghost had been. He sniffed, his dark muzzle questing for the vanished pirate spirit.

I pulled him back to me, hugging him tightly. His muscular body was always reassuring, and the ghost's visit had me shook up a little, even with our pleasant conversation and all.

"I don't know if you understood him," I told Sinbad, "with that English or Irish way of talking. He had to leave because he ran out of energy. In case you don't know it, that was a real ghost. He said he'll be back some other time."

Sinbad looked at me.

"He wants his gold that they cheated him out of when they killed him. I kind of promised to help him find it."

Sinbad sighed and settled back against me. He does that to let me know he's not worried, that he'll protect me.

"Maybe he'll give us some of the gold as a reward, Sinbad. We can always use the money."

Sinbad liked that idea, and kissed me quickly before falling asleep on his favorite pillow. My chest.

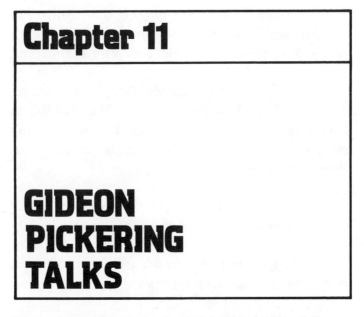

Chapter 11

GIDEON PICKERING TALKS

The next morning at school I tried avoiding Minerva Landry. There was no way I would talk to her about the ghost because she simply wouldn't believe it. I needed facts with her, just as I did with her old man, the Sheriff, and a ghost is no fact, unless you happen to experience one yourself.

She found me anyway. "Solve that kidnapping yet?" she asked cheerfully. "I still haven't heard anything about Gunther Waldorf being missing."

"That's your old man's problem now," I said. "He's the law. I only reported what I happened to see."

"How about that Citizens' Committee for a Cleaner County? Have you discovered any dirty work yet?"

I shook my head, keeping my cool. "Not yet, Minerva. I'll let you know when I discover anything. How about your pop's campaign? Did you tell him he'd better get going with some posters of his own?"

"I told him," she said. "But you know him. He told me not to worry about it. That one election time is just like any other. And if you do your job, people will want you to keep on doing it. You know, like that."

"Rotsa ruck," I said. "Maybe if this Bradley Case gets his job instead, he'll know better too late."

She shrugged. "Well, maybe. But you know you. You're always exaggerating things."

"Okay," I said. "Don't say I didn't warn you."

She waved her hands. "I heard you the second time. What's happening with Mrs. Teska? Have you found out what she's going to do yet with her money when she dies?"

"Not yet," I said. "I'm still working on it."

Minerva grinned and gave me back my own words. "Rotsa ruck."

She added a good stiff punch high on my arm and ran off to class. I'm always surprised at how hard she can hit.

After school I called the office of Mr. Gideon Pickering. His secretary remembered me from the Big Nick Murdock case. When I told her I'd like to discuss something about Mrs. Teska with Mr. Pickering, she said if I came right down there, she would manage to squeeze me in between his appointments.

When I got there, she kept her word. She walked straight to his door, stuck her head in, and came out smiling. "He has another appointment in ten minutes.

Try to be brief." Then she held the door open for me and closed it behind me.

Mr. Pickering looked like one of the men who helped draft our Declaration of Independence. Tall and gaunt, white haired with cold blue eyes, a long-nosed, tough-looking, unsmiling Yankee rebel. He had told me he was eighty years old the last time I saw him, and he didn't look any worse after a year.

He surprised me by getting up from his desk, and leaning across it to shake my hand. "Now we have the formalities done with, Steve, let's get right to it." He took out his old gold watch with the leather and silver fob, and placed it on the desk in front of him.

I stared at the beautiful old watch, as if hypnotized. It had delicate filigree on the gold case, Roman numerals and fluted hands. I licked my lip. "I got ten minutes?"

He nodded and settled back in his high black-leather chair. "More or less," he said. He wore a white shirt buttoned at the collar and a solid black tie. His coat was off and above his thick wrists, I could see pale gold cufflinks. Down below, on Main Street, afternoon traffic hummed.

"I must assume this is a matter of great importance," Mr. Pickering said with his clipped and precise diction, "or you wouldn't have come all the way downtown to see me. Don't let the watch distract you. It's my own reminder to maintain my schedule." Then he leaned forward, his flinty expression softening slightly. "What's troubling you, son?"

"It's about Mrs. Teska," I said. "You remember

her—the old lady with the store on Steamboat Road—
who once was Anna Myszka—Big Nick Murdock's wife
before he had to go away—"

Mr. Pickering nodded to indicate he remembered
her.

"I remember when Big Nick Murdock came back. I
think I heard him say he was going to take care of
Mrs. Teska for her old age." I hesitated. Mrs. Teska had
been an old lady for a long time. "Anyway, what I have
to know is if she has a lot of money now. I mean, did
Big Nick leave her some kind of large inheritance?"

Mr. Pickering looked frostily down his long nose at
me. "I assume you have reason to ask that kind of
question."

"Well, sure. I know it's none of my business. Unless
she happens to have an awful lot. In that case, I got to
be worried because I think somebody in town is trying
a ripoff on her. And you're the only one who would
know because you were his lawyer."

Mr. Pickering looked me over carefully, then picked
his watch off the desk and put it in his pocket. "Some
things go beyond the ordinary importance of time," he
said. "You knew what you were about last time we
met, far beyond your years. Never mind the shortcuts
now. Just give me all your information. Who's doing
the ripoff, how do you know, and so forth."

I told him everything Mrs. Teska had told me. He
listened without interrupting until I was done.

He laced his long white fingers together, frowning.
"As I recall, Mrs. Teska had many old country super-
stitions. There are many instances where gullible or

superstitious people have been taken advantage of by
those who claim to be offering spiritual help. But not
all spiritual advisers are frauds, and sometimes it's
difficult to detect where they are deliberately deceiving
a client. That whole area of the psychic is very mushy,
legally speaking. Very difficult to present evidence in a
court of law inasmuch as demonstrable proof is usually
lacking."

"Well, I don't know about that," I said. "All I know
is she's got this thing now about her dead sister telling her she won't need any money or anything when
she dies. Mrs. Teska is getting herself ready to die soon
to be with her sister, only she's got to give up everything she owns first. I don't want to prove anything
against this guy after she dies. What I want to do is
stop her now before she makes any big mistake either
way."

Mr. Pickering shrugged his wide shoulders. "We can
run a check on the medium to find out if he's legitimate.
Give me that name again."

"Solo Yerkos."

He wrote it down on his yellow lined legal pad. "The
law on fraud and extortion is quite clear. Getting
money under false pretenses is punishable by fine and
sentence. If this man Yerkos has operated illegally
before, there could be a record of his activities. These
people leave a trail behind, and if their victims file a
complaint, they are brought to ground. So Mrs. Teska
can be protected to a certain degree if she is indeed
being swindled of her money. Chances are, she would
get it all back. After the fact, of course. And then, too,

it depends upon how she manages the disposal of her money and property. That is to say, she would be safer if she were to have a proper will drawn to that effect, rather than simply hand her money over on some impulsive arrangement."

"Are you saying she's got a lot of money?"

Mr. Pickering again gave me his deadpan frosty look. "I haven't said anything, young man."

"She told me she's waiting for the final word soon from her sister," I said. "Her store isn't worth too much, I guess, only what if she unloads it now and doesn't die as soon as she thinks?"

Mr. Pickering frowned again, nodding his silvery-white head vigorously. "Well, yes, I can tell you this. Mrs. Teska has a significant amount to lose, if she is persuaded to give it away. Part of it is safeguarded by a trust arranged for her by Mr. Murdock, my client, who did exactly as he promised. He left Mrs. Teska more than enough to see her through any possible contingency in her life. Both in coin of the realm, as we put it, and in valuable real estate."

"Real estate? You mean he left her Captain Billy's castle?"

Mr. Pickering grinned, showing his long straight teeth. "I remember your interest with regard to that house. If it were not for your expertise in old houses, that mystery might never have been solved, would it?"

"Maybe," I said. "But what about it?"

He shook his head. "No, the house goes to the nephew, Defoe."

"The cave, too? You know, the Jonah Jaws."

He nodded, smiling. "Yes, it's part of the house, you see. Not all of Captain Billy Murdock's treasure has been found yet, but in time, young Defoe will dig it up, I'm sure."

Don Defoe was a reporter who worked at the local newspaper. His great-great-grandfather Thomas Defoe was Captain Billy Murdock's first mate, and a brilliant engineer responsible for building the underwater cave that kept everybody out unless they could understand the cipher written high on the cave wall. When Big Nick Murdock came back after I had cleared his name, he decided to break the long-going family feud and welcomed his young nephew Don, starting him off with a fortune.

"I know Big Nick had to leave Mrs. Teska a lot," I said to Mr. Pickering. "What do you mean about it being partly in trust?"

The lawyer smiled. "Exactly what it says, son. Still the old familiar legal professional mumbo jumbo so dearly loved by lawyers, obscure to the general public, but effective in that its precise terms and conditions are clearly stated as to the final disposal and execution of the trust."

I blinked. Mr. Pickering always threw me with his legal high-sounding phrases.

"It means," he said, "that apart from the initial amount my client Mr. Murdock bequeathed to Mrs. Teska, he left a much larger amount, money and property to be held in security for her by a person or institution approved by me as the trustee and executor of Mr. Murdock's estate."

"Like who?" I said.

"The trust fund is held at the Citizens' Bank. The president, E. Biggs Calloway, is an old friend of mine. He is a cotrustee along with me."

"I still don't get how it works in case she wants to give it all away now, like she says she might."

Mr. Pickering shook his head slowly, frowning. "The advantage of the trust fund, you see, is that even if she wants to give the money away, she can't without permission first from Mr. Calloway and me. As cotrustees, he and I decide if the money and trust will be spent sensibly. That's her protection, the way Mr. Murdock meant it to be. Naturally, if we investigate and find this man Yerkos to be a charlatan, we refuse to honor her request, and the funds remain safely in trust."

I got up feeling better about my visit. Mr. Pickering wasn't about to let Mrs. Teska do anything so dumb as to give away her fortune and property just because some wiseapple thought he could play on her emotions and take it away from her.

"That's all I wanted to know," I told Mr. Pickering. "I was afraid she was going to blow a lot of money with this guy."

He spread his hands, looking unhappy. "Well, son, we are still talking about a lot of money here. Apart from the funds and property in trust, Mrs. Teska has an amount equal to one million dollars she can freely draw on her own recognizance."

"A million bucks?" I said, feeling sick. "Does that include some property, too?"

He shook his head. "No, the property is separately

held in trust, but that is well over two million dollars in toto."

I wondered if perhaps Big Nick Murdock had left Mrs. Teska some of his land in Italy where he had been living. "Where is it?"

He tapped the desk with his pencil. "Right off Murdock's castle. Beyond the outer limits of the Jonah Jaws cave, east of Scuttle Point. The entire beach-front, about two miles adjacent to the castle, fronting on the bay. That all belongs to Mrs. Teska now, Steve."

He got up to shake hands, and I thanked him and left feeling dizzy again. The problem I thought solved was now turning into another one.

That beachfront property Mrs. Teska owned now was exactly the area the ghost had told me about. Where he wanted me to dig, to find his gold. And, you know, it's awfully hard to say no to a ghost. Especially one who had been a pirate.

Chapter 12

HOW GIRLS CAN BE A PAIN AND SO FORTH

I was walking Sinbad through the woods near my house later when he began tugging on the leash. He had sensed Minerva Landry a few hundred yards away running down the path toward us. I let Sinbad go and he went off to meet her like a runaway express train. By the time I got there, they had about finished knocking each other around.

"Well, what did Mr. Pickering say about the money?" she asked.

I stared. "How did you know about that?"

"You were avoiding me at school, and later I saw you sneaking off, heading toward town. I know how your head works, and I figured since you hadn't solved anything lately, you'd be heading for the lawyer's office to get some facts about how Mrs. Teska is fixed before you blunder into that case."

"Well, you guessed right. According to Mr. Pickering, Mrs. Teska is really loaded. Big Nick Murdock left her so much you wouldn't believe it."

"Just tell me how much," Minerva said. "I'll believe it."

I gave her the figures Mr. Pickering had given me and her eyes popped. "Wow! Maybe somebody ought to tell her how rich she is, and she could give up her dinky little grocery store."

"She won't be rich too long if that guy Solo Yerkos gets his hands on it."

"Maybe he won't," Minerva said. "All you have to do is tell her to make out a will and leave it with Mr. Pickering, and she'll be protected at least while she's still living."

I shook my head. "It's not what I tell her, Minerva. It's her sister Sofi's spirit she's going to listen to. If you ask me, Big Nick Murdock should have put it all in trust. Then there wouldn't be any problem."

Minerva shrugged. "I know why he did it that way. He knew how old fashioned Mrs. Teska is, and how it would be too much of a hassle for her to go through that trustee business anytime she needed money. So he left her some loose money around to have fun with."

"Maybe you ought to tell your pop about it," I said. "If Yerkos knows how much she has, he might find some way of getting it all. That's three million dollars— not counting all that pirate gold buried on her beach property."

Minerva cocked her head. "What pirate gold?"

"Who said anything about pirate gold?" I said, realizing my mistake too late.

She punched me on the arm. "You did. What's that all about?"

Sinbad was looking up at me. "Well, I don't know it for a fact," I said lamely. "It's only what the ghost told me."

"A ghost? You saw a ghost?"

She was beginning to crack up, laughing, and so I got mad and told her about it. "He looked like a regular ghost, you know, sort of transparent. You can see right through them. Except for the fact that I could see he was a pirate."

"I think your head is transparent, and somebody can see right through to the empty place your brains should be. How do you get to dream all this stuff up?"

"Sinbad was there. He's a witness," I said. "You don't have to take my word for it."

She looked down at Sinbad. "I don't know. Maybe you've trained him to tell lies for you. So what about all this pirate gold. I guess this ghost lost it. Is that your story?"

"You'll see, if I ever find it," I said. "He said it's gold they looted and plundered from a Spanish ship."

Minerva was smiling, shaking her head, then tapping it with her finger as if I'd lost my senses. So I told her everything the ghost had said on his visit. Minerva listened carefully until I was finished.

"I would hate myself if I believed this story," she said. "You say this pirate ghost came to see you about helping him get his share of the gold? What's he going to do with it, even supposing you get lucky enough to find it? He's dead, isn't he? He knows that, doesn't he? And forgetting those questions for a moment, why you?

How come he picked you out of all the people living around here?"

"I asked the same questions, Minerva. About what he's going to do with it, he said he'll tell me later. About why he picked me, he said I was responsible for stirring up his ectoplasm—that's like his energy—and while at first he seemed mad about that, then he took a fancy to Sinbad and me, too, I guess, and decided we could help him."

"How could you stir up his ectoplasm? You don't know anything about ghost raising."

"I know. But Herky was explaining to me all there was to know about ghosts and spirits, psychics and so on. I guess that's what he meant about getting the vibrations."

She shrugged. "I didn't know they were that sensitive."

"Well, he said something else—that it was something in the air over that beach area near where the gold is buried. Some vibrations. So it wasn't all my fault, or Herky's."

"Did he tell you where it was buried? I mean, how many fathoms deep, like they do, and how many paces from the old oak stump, north by northeast, and all that pirate-jazz talk?"

"It was buried in a cave, he said. Only the hills came down during the years, and it's buried now—the cave, that is—and he can't tell exactly where it is. Only on the beach somewhere around Scuttle Point. West to about here."

"Terrific," she said. "That means you'll only have

about two miles of beach to dig up. That should take you about a couple of hundred years. Maybe you'll be a ghost yourself by that time, and you'll be visiting people later on in their bedrooms, scaring the wits out of them, telling them you're looking for the gold, and would they like to help." She laughed. "It will be like a ghost chain letter."

"Very funny," I said. "Only I promised to help him. I know it sounds crazy but even though he scared me, I felt sorry for him. You know, being a ghost and all, having to hang around the place where they killed him all these years, guarding the treasure he can't find anymore."

"You're the one who's crazy. You don't have to believe everything he says, do you? Why does he have to hang around, if he's tired of it? If I were a ghost, I'd travel all over the world. Think about that—a free trip!"

"Ghosts can't cross water—according to Captain Marion, anyway. He ought to know."

"Maybe," she said. "Did he tell you why they killed him?"

"It sounded like they double-crossed him. It was supposed to be equal shares for the crew over the plunder. The next thing he knew, they'd killed him, and his ghost was supposed to guard the treasure. So he's been doing that, on and off, almost two hundred years, he said."

Minerva shook her head, sending her long blond hair flying. "I think you and your ghost will make a perfect pair. You're always inventing stories you can't prove, and here is your ghost walking around his treasure all this time and now he forgets where they put it."

"Don't forget the hills came down."

"Well, even so, what happened to that famous pirate 'X marks the spot' jazz? Another thing that's wrong with your story is that pirates always had a map of their hidden treasure. How come he didn't have one?"

"I don't know. I guess he figured as long as he would always be around, why would he need a map?"

"Well, tell him next time you see him that now he knows why. So he can locate his treasure. And one more thing, before I forget, did this Captain Marion tell you how much he would pay you if you found the gold? You know, equal shares, or whatever."

"No, we didn't get into that, Minerva. If you ever talk to a ghost, you'll find out it's not easy to think about everything. They kind of blow your mind."

"I think you lost yours long ago, so you can't blame that on him. Also you might tell him next time he comes out of your woodwork, that in all this time some-body else might have found the gold. Especially if he's been goofing off, not guarding it all the time, until now he can't even remember where it is."

"I don't think he'd like hearing that. He looks as if he had a real mean temper once. And he wears a band-age over one eye. I guess somebody got him in a fight."

"Well, you don't know that, either, for sure, do you? Maybe he just put that on to scare you."

"He did all right without that, but it helped. What's your guess about how much gold is really there in that cave? You know, considering that those old Spanish ships carried a lot of gold and silver."

"My guess? I'd say about five percent of nothing. You still don't know where it is, or if it's still there, dumbbell."

"Okay, you had your chance. I was going to cut you in on some of my reward, but no more." I turned to Sinbad. "Remember that, we don't give her a nickel."

Minerva laughed. She leaned over to sock Sinbad. "I feel sorry for you, Sinbad, having to live with such a dumb master. But if that ghost ever comes back, and you want a place to hide out, you can always stay with me."

With that, she took off, leaving Sinbad staring and whining. Then he looked up at me, and I had the weird feeling that he was considering her offer.

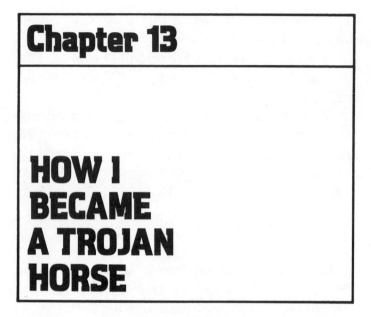

Chapter 13

HOW I BECAME A TROJAN HORSE

I wanted to talk to Mrs. Teska some more, especially about the idea of her making out a will, as Minerva Landry and Mr. Pickering had suggested. But she had the CLOSED sign in her door window again. She could have been upstairs in her apartment over the store resting, but I decided not to disturb her, and instead continued on my bike to the new village at the far end of town. There wasn't anything I could think of doing about the Gunther Waldorf problem, and I didn't have any solution to Mrs. Teska's, either, and the new Citizens' Committee was all that was left for me to investigate. If I could prove they were a crooked outfit, then perhaps I might get Sheriff Landry stirred up to start his own campaign. Then maybe things would get rolling.

A big white banner floated high across Main Street downtown carrying their name and slogan. One end was attached to the roof of a store in the middle of the block. Over the store was a large canvas sign. CITIZENS' COMMITTEE FOR A CLEANER COUNTY.

I got off my bike and looked in through the store window. It appeared to be their headquarters, with a lot of activity going on inside. I wanted to go in there and find out how they operated, but I couldn't think of a good excuse. Then I noticed a small sign stuck in the corner of the window.

> BOYS AND GIRLS WANTED
> Ages 11 to 16
> Part-time work
> after school and Saturdays.
> Earn $25 a week and more.
> Apply inside to Miss Hale.
> Citizens' Committee for a Cleaner County.

I felt like cheering. Here was the way to find out things about this outfit. To work from the inside, like a super spy.

Like the Trojan horse.

The old Greeks had fooled the Trojans, a super race, with it—that strange gift left outside their gates after the Greek army retreated, which the Trojans were dumb enough to take inside. They never suspected it contained an assault group of Greek soldiers who broke out later and overpowered the guards, opened the gates, and let the Greek army in to take the city.

Hooray, I told myself. It's our chance for a big breakthrough. Now you can find out firsthand whether this bunch is on the level or not. Maybe you can prove to Sheriff Landry you're not so crazy after all.

Through the store window, I could see the floor crammed with desks, with men and women at them typing, or using the phones. Others were working mimeographing machines, stacking up piles of circulars.

Near the front window a table was covered with posters and different stacks of circulars, and I saw they weren't out for only Sheriff Landry's job as sheriff and police chief. They had their own people up for all the local offices, councilman, supervisor, judge, treasurer, and mayor. There were faces I didn't know on the photos, names I didn't recognize.

They acted organized and efficient, going about it, it seemed, as if they were planning a war. It amounted to that, it seemed to me, because if they got into power, the people of Hampton would have to live under their authority.

If Minerva was right about them not being crooks, and I was way off, it wouldn't hurt for me to find that out, too, so I wouldn't go around afterward labeled as the village idiot.

In that case I would have to come up with a new theory for the kidnapping of Gunther Waldorf. Nobody but me thought a crime had taken place there. But now a way had been provided for me to investigate, to stop shooting off my mouth, and start using other faculties I had, like my ears, eyes, and brains.

Nobody paid any attention to me as I walked inside. The typewriters clacked like machine guns. Phones were ringing on almost every desk, like a concert. I walked the entire length of the store without anybody grabbing me and yelling, "Stop, spy!"

At the rear were small partitions for offices. I stopped short at the first one. A pale-faced man in white shirtsleeves sat beside a desk. The new candidate for office, the sheriff-to-be, he hoped—Bradley Case. I knew I couldn't be wrong about that long thin nose, the dark, closely set eyes, the long jutting jaw.

A woman with short blond hair was sitting behind the desk. There were papers piled all over it and three telephones. She was picking up one of the phones when she saw me. Hanging up, she beckoned me closer.

"I'm Miss Hale," she said. "Are you here for the part-time work delivering posters?"

I nodded and stepped through the open doorway. Bradley Case glanced at me in a detached way, and lit a long cigar.

Miss Hale glanced down at a sheet of paper and a map of the Hampton district. "What end of town do you live at?"

I waved my hand toward the northeast. "The Point."

"Hm," she said. "Old Village. We need more coverage there." She looked me over and nodded. "Well, you look strong enough. Those posters weigh a lot, you know. You may have to carry two sacks."

"That's okay," I said.

She circled her pencil over the map. I stepped closer and looked down at various circles drawn in color all over our village and the immediate outlying suburbs. Her pencil stopped at a patch without any marked circles. "Do you know where Maple Street is?"

"Yes, ma'am."

She smiled and made a mark on the map. "Good. You'll find Mr. Rally out there now, outside the park at the corner of Stoner. That's the drop-off area for the circulars where you'll pick up with the other kids. What's your name?"

"Steve Forrester."

She wrote my name quickly on a small piece of paper, and then her name underneath. Handing it to me, she said, "Tell Mr. Rally Miss Hale sent you. The pay is one dollar an hour. When you run out, if Mr. Rally has nothing left, report back here tomorrow. And thanks for dropping by, Steve."

When I turned to go, she was telling Bradley Case about some dense areas in the old village they had to saturate. He nodded with a tired expression, puffing slowly on his cigar. His shoulders were slumped and he looked really beat.

I made a mental note to tell Sheriff Landry that the way Bradley Case looked now, he might be too tired to do anything after election day. But meanwhile I had to get on my bike and meet up with Mr. Rally at the park.

I figured that the more I came back to the store headquarters for the campaign, the more I could discover about the new Citizens' Committee and what they were up to. I could pass on this information to Sheriff Landry. If he didn't get reelected, it wasn't going to be my fault. Meanwhile, a dollar an hour wasn't bad for easy part-time work.

I had to admit Miss Hale seemed like a decent, bright person, not a sneaky-looking conniving type. Like the other women I had noticed working there, all nice on the surface. It made me worry a little about why I was so certain this new Citizens' Committee was a bunch of crooks. Maybe I was trying too hard to fit a fact into a wrong theory.

It's okay, I told myself, as I pedaled along, maybe something will turn up, and you'll be right, after all. One little visit doesn't prove anything. Besides, they're on the wrong side, as far as I'm concerned, and it's like a war. Sheriff Landry needs all the soldiers like me he can get.

It took me about ten minutes to get to the park. A man up on an open-back Chevy pickup truck was tossing bound stacks of circulars to the sidewalk. A small group of kids about my age were breaking open the tied bundles and separating them into individual piles.

When the man jumped down, I handed him the slip from Miss Hale. "Okay, Steve. Take what you can carry for King's Point. Be sure you get some of each up."

He handed me two cloth sacks and a roll of tape, and showed me how to select the posters from the piles. There was one for each candidate with his or her picture and the offices they were running for, in bold black type.

I skimmed a thick stack from of each of the five piles, including Bradley Case, and shoved them into the canvas sacks. They were heavy, and when I pushed off on my bike, I wobbled like crazy fighting for balance.

"Maybe you have too much there," Mr. Rally said.

"It's okay," I said stubbornly. "I can handle it."

He shrugged, and I wheeled off, swaying wildly, trying to adjust to the weight of the sacks on my handle-bars. The other kids were heading off with their own sackloads following the routes planned for us by Mr. Rally. Mine was my own home section, Steamboat Road up to and around the Point. I was hoping that when Sheriff Landry saw all the new posters up around him, he would catch on to the kind of organization the Citizens' Committee had going for them. Then, maybe, he would get his own party going before it got snowed under.

I stopped at every corner along the route sticking up this poster and that, changing the candidates as I went along. After a while I looked back and saw the row of white posters hanging in my wake, like seeds I had planted, and I began to feel rotten and sorry I had ever thought of this dopey idea.

I didn't know any more about what kind of organization Sheriff Landry had behind him than I did about the Citizens' Committee, whether they were good or bad. The truth was that I didn't know anything about local politics, about what was going on right in my own hometown. Most of the kids my age didn't, either. We left that stuff to our parents, and the other grown-ups, the ones who voted.

I made up my mind that after I got rid of the posters, I was going to try to find out what was happening, like how to tell a good candidate from a bad one, and so on. And in the meantime, I thought Sheriff Landry, trusting the democratic process as much as he did, was pushing his luck too far.

Meanwhile I was fighting the upgrade of Steamboat Road, pedaling into a stiff cold wind that brought tears to my eyes. My ears were numb. My nose was frozen and my hands were turning blue. I was beginning to wonder what was so terrific about my idea of being a Trojan horse.

After a while I got past my own section and up to the bay area near the Landry house, and the larger estates along the water. I stopped at each block and put up a sign.

I was off my bike and putting up one more, when I heard a car hum along the back bay road, slow down, and stop. I was too cold to stop and see who it might be. All I wanted to do now was get rid of all the dumb posters, put them all up, empty my sacks, and get on home where it would be nice and warm.

I taped it up, and turned back to my bike. The car was still there. There wasn't anything I could do now. Sheriff Landry was staring bleakly across the narrow road at the poster for Bradley Case I had put up.

He didn't say anything, and neither did I. I adjusted the heavy green canvas sacks, and pedaled away.

I had already got rid of about half the posters, and the remaining load should have been lighter, much easier to handle. Instead, it felt heavier. I felt the same way inside, loaded with guilt.

I knew then that my idea of becoming a Trojan horse wasn't as great as I had thought. To get any satisfaction from it, you had to have your friends know you were a friend, not an enemy.

Chapter 14

SOLO YERKOS, THE SOUPED-UP PSYCHIC

Mrs. Teska's store had the OPEN sign out Saturday morning but I didn't have time to talk to her. I was due back at the Citizens' Committee headquarters store to follow up on my Trojan horse plan. When I got there, the typing and phones were already going full blast, although it was early in the day. Miss Hale smiled at me and asked how many hours I had worked for Mr. Rally. Two, I told her, and she handed me two dollars.

"Next time," she said, "have Mr. Rally make out a voucher slip for you. Did he tell you to report back to him after you finished?"

I told her no, he didn't.

She smiled thinly. "Mr. Rally isn't well organized yet. But if you're interested in working again, you'll find him out at the east bay area this morning." She checked a blown-up wall map and put her finger on it. "The corner of Cove and Bay."

I said I knew where that was, and she smiled and said how helpful it was to have a new boy who knew his way around Hampton. I couldn't tell her I didn't mean to be helpful, that I was really a secret spy hoping to uncover something crooked about her organization that I could pass along to Sheriff Landry.

As I went out, two men were coming in, strangers to me. One was sandy haired, short, chunky with a pot-belly. The other was a real big guy about a foot taller with a dented nose. With his tough-looking, rugged features and powerful build, he could have been an ex-pro football tackle or linebacker. With crime on my mind, I figured the chunky one to be part of the top brass of the organization, and the big guy his body-guard.

The bodyguard had the door open for the chunky man. "Miss Hale has all the dope you need, Mr. Calloway. She's got a breakdown of the county inch by inch."

The chunky Calloway had a growling rasp to his voice. "She better have, Joe. Time's running short. We've got to go all out."

The door closed behind them and I unlocked my bike. Suddenly a tape replay flipped on inside my head. Mr. Gideon Pickering was speaking. "The trust fund is held at the Citizens' Bank. The president, E. Biggs Calloway, is an old friend of mine. He is a cotrustee along with me."

There was something wrong. The short, chunky Calloway didn't look anywhere near Mr. Pickering's age. He was more like forty, closer to Sheriff Landry's.

I pedaled out to Cove and Bay. It's at the far end of town. Nothing much around but boatyards strung along the bay, an oil refinery, and Mucker's Swamp. The swamp is a network of twisting, tarry creeks connecting with the sea. It looks bad and smells worse.

Mr. Rally was with another bunch of kids, dealing out the stacks of poster circulars. I told him what Miss Hale had said about the voucher slip. He said if I returned after emptying my sacks, he would take care of it. "But that's dumb," he said. "By the time you get rid of them, you'll be up near Jonah's Bay. You'd have to come all the way back, and I won't be around then. That woman down there ain't organized. Why don't you just grab a big load now that will take about two hours to hang up, and I'll sign the slip for you right now."

It sounded good, and I loaded up. He mapped my route. West to the estates and north to the bay. He signed the voucher for two hours in advance.

I hit the streets, sticking the posters to the big timber telephone poles. This bay area off the swamp was an eyesore, with nautical supply shops, body repair shops, a few gas stations, and a junkyard. The houses nearby were small with scruffy yards. It was the backwater part of Hampton most people never saw, the grubbier side. If the new Citizens' Committee wanted to do a cleanup on our town, this was a good place to start.

My sacks were getting lighter, and I headed for the bluffs, the hilly part of Hampton overlooking Jonah's Bay. Sea captains had lived ashore here in the old days. Many of the older houses had the Captain's Walk, a white parapet, on the roof. The streets were short and narrow, some with the original cobblestones.

You could read Hampton's nautical history by looking at the street signs: Shrike, Crow's Nest, Hurricane, Frigate, King's Way, Yardarm, Union Jack, Privateer, Westwind, Yawl.

I kept going like a robot, mechanically putting up the posters. When I looked back, I could see them flapping in the breeze, each one reminding me of how I was helping the opposition instead of Sheriff Landry. You dope, I told myself, how could you talk yourself into this?

But I had to stick with my plan, dumb as it seemed now, and soon I came to the corner of Reef and Galleon with only five circulars left. Till then I had been sticking them on anything that would hold, the telephone poles, fences, or gateposts. Now with just the few left, I looked around to finish the job with a flourish.

I was in front of an eighteenth-century Flemish Colonial with a "Dutch kick" roof, and wide-flared gambrel overhang, one of our prize architectural relics built by the early Flemish settlers, who used its design all over Long Island where they first settled. The chimney was inside the wall, the fireplace back not showing in the gable end. I was so mad at myself I couldn't enjoy looking at it this day. I stuck Jane Penny for Treasurer up on its gate post.

Sheldon S. Pry for Supervisor was next in my hand. I put him on the picket fence of an 1820 saltbox on Reef Street. Across the street was a big sycamore with a birdhouse spreading its shade over an old Cape Cod with a "rainbow roof." I always liked its curved flare but this time I stuck John Loot for Judge on the sycamore and pedaled off fast without a second look.

With two posters left, I went up Galleon and its smooth timeworn cobblestones. It had a terrific 1860 Victorian with its original octagonal mansard roof still intact on a three-story tower. I had spent days outside with my pop making sketches of its arched Roman dormers, fishscale slates, decorated parapets, Moorish arches, and intricate iron cresting. Today it was just another old building and Alden Bloodletter for Mayor went on its gate.

I took out the one poster remaining, a Bradley Case for Sheriff. I wanted a special place for this one, to round it all off right. The last street along the bay cliff front was Hellsfire. The end house on the high bluff was isolated, a two-story red clapboard-over-timber Garrison Colonial dating back to the year 1700. It was called the "Old King Dick house" and had been boarded up for years.

It was a house with a grisly history based on all kinds of rumors. It had witnessed a murder, a suicide, and a visiting headless apparition carrying his head in his hands, still searching for his killer, as the story went. Whether true or not, the stories made the old Colonial hard to rent or sell. But then for the first time in my life I saw smoke curling up from its end chimneys, and

I stopped. Who would be brave enough to live in the Old King Dick house?

Like all Colonials, it was small, the long side parallel to the street. It looked neglected, needing paint and repair. Steep sloping gables merged into built-in end chimneys. The windows were large with small 12-over-12 lights, one in each end gable. Five windows above and below on the side, four in front. The sashes sagged. The porch, a later addition, was off center. Over the transom were four arched tombstone lights, earmarks of its early date. Plain pilasters flanked the paneled door.

Those were the details, what you saw looking at the old house. But my pop had told me many times that houses were always telling you what they were about, and you had to do more than see, you had to listen, as well, and finally you had to feel. You had to break through the trees and grass and flowers, the trimmings, he called them, and concentrate on the design and material of the house. It was like you were meditating to get an understanding of the feelings surrounding the house, its own particular vibrations.

I wasn't too good at it.

A house is retiring, he would say, like a saltbox, or grand like a Georgian, or preening like a Victorian with everything in the world on it, or dignified like a Tudor, stuffy like a Federal, or proud as a Colonial.

Well, I told him, the people built the house. Are you talking about the vibrations of the house or the people living inside? He said it was a little of both. The people took on some of the characteristics of the house, and vice versa.

I closed my eyes. Okay, house, I muttered, tell me

something about yourself. I heard the wind sighing through the pines. Broken shutters slapping gently against the faded red clapboards. Boards creaking, dry of sap and stretched to their limit. I heard gulls scream-ing in the sky and the roar of surf breaking on the shore below the bluffs a hundred yards north of the house.

The house looked desolate and sickly because it needed repair. But although it was in a bleak setting, it gave out no overtones of evil. It was just another house with a history sitting there waiting for something to happen again.

I kept stalling around hoping to find out who was living here. The gate needed a paint job and was missing a couple of pickets. The serpentine walk needed grading and more flagstones. The hedges weren't trimmed, and the lawn wanted sodding. The flowerbeds were long dead, cluttered with fallen leaves. I had to wonder if the interior of the Garrison was as rundown and neglected. It could mean a job for my pop.

A metal mailbox hung on a low pitted wood post. I moved closer to read the name of the new occupant and my eyes froze.

Solo Yerkos!

I stepped back, startled. I needed to know when he had moved in here, and how recently Mrs. Teska had begun coming over. If Yerkos got some of Mrs. Teska's money, he could fix up this place. There was an ex-tension in the back, outbuildings, a shed and barn, all falling apart. Honest or not, he would need a lot of money to put this place in order.

Then I saw parked back on the rutted driveway, a

black Continental. The same snazzy late model that had nearly run me over as it zoomed down the gravel driveway of Gunther Waldorf. I could imagine the look on Sheriff Landry's face when I told him I had spotted the mystery getaway car, and now what was he going to do about the Gunther Waldorf kidnap caper.

Ducking low, I went around the gate to avoid being seen from inside the house. The license plate numbers were still stuck in my head. NK 3163. If this plate matched, I would have the kind of fact Sheriff Landry liked.

But another few steps up the driveway and my hopes went glimmering. The car plate was JP 8910. I shook my head, disappointed and unbelieving. It had to be the same car. But a fact is a fact, and it was only when I turned away and saw the long thin scratch on the left .front fender that I was sure again I was right. I hadn't told Sheriff Landry about it because I forgot I had noticed it when they zoomed by. But I saw it again now in my mind's eye, the long marring scratch on the sparkling new left fender as I was struggling to get my bike out of the way.

Then I sensed somebody watching me. I turned and saw a man on the front porch, the door open behind him. The wheels spun slowly inside my head as I tried to think of a good excuse for trespassing on the property.

He stepped off the porch. He was tall and thin with dark hair falling over his collar. His face was pale and gaunt with dark, deep-set eyes. He looked like an actor, and his voice was deep and resonant like one. "You, there! What are you doing on this property?"

I looked down at my hands and saw with a sigh of relief they were holding the last poster. I had been so interested in the house, I had forgotten about hanging the poster. "It's this new poster for the Citizens' Committee," I said glibly, crossing the driveway toward him, holding it up for him to read. "One of their people running for office. They hired me to stick these around town, and I was looking for a good place here to display it."

That excuse sounded pretty good to me but one look at his face told me he didn't buy it. He shook his head, smiling thinly, his black eyes boring into mine. "No, that's not it—not quite," he said.

He walked slowly toward me with a languid gait. His eyes stayed riveted on mine. He stopped a few feet away, cocked his head, and closed his eyes. "Ah—I see numbers. NK 3163. You are thinking of those exact numbers. Correct?"

I stared, shaken by his words. How did he read my mind? I tried to get all the numbers out of my head. Maybe if I talked fast, I thought, he would lose the connection with what was going on inside me. "N-no, sir," I stammered. "I'm just trying to find a good place for this last poster." I looked wildly around, and pointed off. "Maybe that big oak off to the side would be okay, if you don't mind."

He was smiling, shaking his head negative. Again his black eyes fastened on mine, and I felt myself getting weaker, as if he were draining something out of me. I tried to block my mind, to think of other things. I thought of eating, which I'm generally good at, but

I couldn't even come up with a hamburger. I thought of swimming, but it was too cold, and I thought of running but I was too tired, all of a sudden, and then I wished Sinbad was with me so that I wouldn't feel scared.

Yerkos nodded. "No, your dog would not help you."

I looked at him, stricken dumb, feeling awfully helpless.

"A short, squat animal," he said. "Very powerful. And ugly, one might think."

I came out of his spell. "He's an English bulldog, yeah."

His lips pursed. "Yes, that is so. About this poster, you may hang it or not. But you must forget this silly notion about the other man. He is not here."

"Other man?" I echoed, dazed. How did he do that?

He chopped the air with the side of his hand. "Please, young man, Solo Yerkos does not play silly games. What is your name?"

"Steve Forrester."

He nodded and cocked his head to the side again, looking past me. "Yes, that is so. Let me see—what else you are concerning yourself about." His eyes zapped into mine again, and I actually felt the force of his intense gaze. It was almost like a blow pushing me back a step. I held my breath and tried to make my mind blank, to seal up every secret I had from him.

His body became rigid for a long moment. Then he exhaled and nodded as if satisfied. "Ah! So that is it! I thought there was more to this visit."

"Huh?" I said, wondering what he had seen inside me now.

He was turning away. "It is the old woman, eh? Mrs. Teska." His glance over his shoulder mocked me. "You need not concern yourself about her."

I stared at him.

He lifted his chin, and then snapped his long white fingers. "She will know what she has to do soon enough. There is nothing you can do."

He turned his back on me then, and walked to his house. The door opened and closed. He was gone, and as the old Colonial door closed behind him, I shivered.

When I recovered my senses, I got on my bike and pedaled away fast. Then I saw I was still holding on to that dumb poster of Bradley Case for sheriff.

I ripped it in half, and then into quarters, and then into small pieces. Then I threw all the pieces up in the air like confetti and watched behind me as the wind blew them away.

After that, I rode on home, more than a little scared. I still didn't know what Solo Yerkos was up to with Mrs. Teska, but I did know that whatever he decided to do, he was going to be a very tough man to stop.

And when I thought about the idea of me being the one who was going to do it, it seemed kind of ridiculous. Unless I was able to find a way to go around without an exposed mind showing.

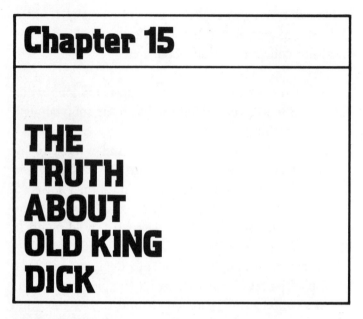

Chapter 15

THE TRUTH ABOUT OLD KING DICK

Herky looked happy to see me. He listened to my story about seeing Solo Yerkos and having my mind probed, with sparkling eyes, looking excited instead of sympathetic. I always forget that what interests Herky most is the problem.

"Apparently Solo Yerkos has strong occult and psychic powers, Steve. What you probably didn't know is that supposedly every thought we have takes on a certain form. It hangs in the air like an astral picture which psychics can see. There was no way you could have hidden or blocked out what you were thinking, if that makes you feel any better."

"It doesn't," I said. "Because now I'm sure that he is going to rip off Mrs. Teska. He can use her money. That place he lives in is the early Garrison Colonial called the Old King Dick house, and it's falling apart."

Herky blinked and whistled. "Is that what it's called? Wow! That's terrific!"

"What's so terrific about it?" I said. "I guess he was the original owner, Old King Dick, the guy who first built it way back in 1700."

Herky shook his head. "I'm afraid that isn't what it means at all, Steve. 'Old King Dick' is an old English expression. One of many names they have for the Devil."

I stared at him. "Old King Dick means the Devil?"

He nodded. "They had many words for the Devil. There was the Black Man, or Black Peter, Black Tom, Blackthorn, the Old Man, the bogeyman, the wolf, and the fox. Old King Dick was another word for Satan, Lucifer, the Devil, and I hope you're not thinking what I am."

I shook my head. "No way. I'll agree Solo Yerkos is probably some kind of powerful psychic. But he's not the Devil."

Herky grinned. "Did he have eyes like saucers, which squinted terribly, and struck out sparks of blue fire when he winked? Did his eyelids chatter like flints or struck steel?"

"No, I think mine were the ones chattering. He just lays this look on you, and next thing you know your brains are coming apart to let his mind-reading beam scan what's going on in there."

Herky frowned. "He could be a black magician. Meaning, he could influence your thinking, or anybody's, to do what he wanted. Don't kid yourself. That kind of concentration in the wrong mind can even kill people."

"That's all I have to hear, Herk. How come you're so cheerful today?"

"I'm not trying to frighten you, Steve. You've told me how he has already begun to influence Mrs. Teska. And the incident involving you shows his occult power. He may be a magician, witch, or warlock. We have to consider, as well, the fact that whether by accident or design, he's living in a house named after the Devil."

"Okay, I'm considering everything you said. But it still doesn't help because I know I have to do something."

"You can't save Mrs. Teska by yourself, Steve. You're overmatched."

"I know that. It's why I came over to see you. Last time you offered to loan me your supernatural occult books but I didn't think I'd need them. I've changed my mind."

"You don't seem to understand," Herky said patiently. "The books cover the full range of psychic phenomena. Reading them won't do you any good unless you had psychic power yourself. What you need is an occult counterthrust. Some other strong magician or psychic who can blunt the power of the Devil manifest in Solo Yerkos."

"That's a neat idea, Herk. Except that I don't know anybody like that. That old attorney Gideon Pickering told me the law could stop Yerkos only if he's on record for having defrauded people before. And if they were willing to file a complaint against him. Otherwise, he's free to operate any way he likes."

Herky's black eyes were snapping, his pale skin

flushed. He snapped his fingers. "Well, there's Dark Cloud, you know."

"Dark Cloud? Who's he?"

"The Shinnecock *shaman*—their legendary medicine man."

He looked serious, and I could feel my insides cheering up. "Hey, George Cooper, that kid in our school, is a Shinnecock, isn't he?"

Herky was reaching for the telephone book. "He and his family live off the reservation, you know. But George might be willing to do a favor for us."

"He would? That sounds terrific, but how come? I mean, I like George but I don't know him that well."

Herky had the page he wanted in the phone book. "He might do it. His old man is a big shot with the United Indian Development Association, a past president of internal affairs."

I stared at him, puzzled. "So what?"

Herky picked up the phone and began dialing. "My mother works on that Internal Affairs Committee."

I didn't know how important that would be to Dark Cloud. But Herky was already talking into the phone. "Hello, George. This is Herky Krakower. Listen, I wonder if you could do me a small favor. You would? Hey, that's terrific. Steve Forrester is here now and—"

Chapter 16

DARK CLOUD AND HIS GREAT SPIRIT

The Shinnecock tribal reservation is outside of town along the waters of the South Inner Bay. It's one of the authentic attractions on Long Island, one of the few instances in our history where we haven't displaced the native Americans from their original stamping ground.

George Cooper was waiting for me outside the reservation near the big sign telling everybody who could read that this land belonged to the Shinnecock nation. George is my age, stocky like me, blessed with no hangups and a nice sense of humor.

He raised his hand in a mock greeting, TV style. "How?" he said.

I patted my 10-speeder. "Pedal power, George. That's how. I forgot what a long ride it was. Sorry if I kept you waiting."

"It's okay," he said. "It gave me a little time to look around the place. I haven't visited in years. My old man got out of here a long time ago and wants everybody to do the same. Into the melting pot, he says. But I know he also doesn't ever want me to forget where I'm coming from."

"Sounds reasonable," I said. "Did Herky tell you why I needed this favor about seeing Dark Cloud?"

"He didn't go into it much, Steve. But it's okay, because in a way you'll be doing me a favor."

"How come?"

George thumbed his chest. "I'm related to Dark Cloud. His great-great-great grandson, I think. He's very old, about ninety-two, and I don't think he'll remember me, but it gives me a good excuse to see him again. He may have lost some of his powers but it won't matter—he's still terrific."

I didn't want to go into about how much power Dark Cloud had lost because I needed all the help I could get. I followed George as he wheeled his bike inside the big open gate. I had been there before with my old man, and the reservation hadn't changed. They had prefab housing, one- and two-story apartment units, a large central council meeting house of cement blocks, and a playground with a lot of little kids running around, climbing through obstacle tunnels, playing on seesaws, and going up and down a long slide into a sandbox.

TV antennas dotted every roof, and cars were parked in open carports and driveways. Kids about our age were hanging around, some playing ball. They looked curiously at us but George ignored them and we kept going to the far end.

"Do you think Dark Cloud will do the reading for me, George? And also does he charge a lot?"

George shrugged. "I can't promise he'll do it for you. But if he does, he won't charge you anything. He's one of our legendary great medicine men with a remarkable gift for prophecy. But he's cooled on it. He hasn't been happy with the modernization and assimilation of the Shinnecocks, and he's been silent for many years. It's as if he's retired, given up his spiritual powers."

"It sounds like he's against progress."

George shook his head. "No, it's not that. He's a very religious man, and we all kind of got away from that. He's against the hunt for money, greed, commercialism —all the trimmings of modern society."

"I don't even know what to ask him," I said.

"The way I understand it," George said, "you don't have to worry about that. Dark Cloud will tell you what you have to know, anyway."

"It all started when this new Citizens' Committee began spreading their posters around, offering their own candidates for election. Since then, a lot of weird things have happened."

"Yeah, I know about them," George said. "It's another reason I came with you. My old man majored in political science. He knows the score about how new political parties can take over. Sometimes they chisel away at Indian rights and reservation land. It's called eco-raiding. And he's not about to let our people here wind up sleeping behind garbage cans. So he's looking to see if this new committee is out to take the noble red man one more time."

"Maybe Dark Cloud can use his magic for that," I said.

George Cooper shook his head negative. "He wouldn't use his sacred spirits for any political junk. It would offend his spirits. That stuff is for our legal council to fight. But if you have a personal problem, Dark Cloud might help you. It's up to how important he thinks it is, and if he thinks you're a worthwhile person. Dark Cloud wouldn't waste his time or that of the Great Spirit on anything trivial."

I got the worrisome thought that Dark Cloud would take one look at me and say, "Hey, get this dopey kid out of here. I wouldn't want to waste a single spirit on his dumb case. Look at what happened to us poor Indians if he thinks that *he's* got a problem."

"I don't know if my problem is important enough for Dark Cloud," I said, "but it's got me worried. There's a kidnapping I saw that nobody else believes happened. And a new psychic moved into town and I think is trying a ripoff on an old woman I know. That's apart from my friend Sheriff Landry losing his job if the new committee sweeps the election."

George smiled and tugged at my arm. "Hey, come on. I'm kind of interested in all this myself. Maybe Dark Cloud will respond. Remember, I don't know any more about tribal magic than you do."

He led me around to an outer path leading to separate frame cottages. We parked our bikes and

George knocked on the door. There wasn't any answer. George looked up at the sun. "He may be around the back sunning."

We circled the small house and George pointed to the others ringing that of Dark Cloud. "Those are for the other old tribal chiefs," he said. "They're all kind of special and keep to themselves. They don't mix with the younger element."

A large craggy man was sitting like a stone statue gazing into the sky, eyes squinted against the sun. George walked up to him slowly, stood quietly in front of him, and bowed his head respectfully.

"Greetings, grandfather Dark Cloud. I am George, the great-great-great grandson. My father is David Angry Runner. He does the reading of the law for the people."

The old man lifted his massive chest and a long sigh escaped him. He must have been an awesome figure in his day. At ninety-two, he was still powerful looking. Broad shoulders, thick arms. His long straight gray hair fell to his shoulders. His leathery, craggy face carried a million wrinkles. "Angry Runner," the old man said softly, as if to himself.

"He's the son of Straight Path who was the son of—"

Dark Cloud held up his huge hand and George stopped. "Enough. You are all my sons." His narrowed iron-gray eyes shifted to mine.

"This is Steve Forrester, a friend. He is in need of a prayer to the Divine Spirit, grandfather."

Dark Cloud's eyes closed. He opened them again and

looked at me intently. They locked on mine, unblinking and steady.

I decided what I ought to do was tell him all about Mrs. Teska and her problem with the medium Solo Yerkos, giving up her life and her money. Then I thought maybe I ought to throw in the part about the big Lincoln zooming out of the driveway on Tupelo Lane with Gunther Waldorf in the back seat between two men. While you're at it, I told myself, maybe you should mention Sheriff Landry, so you'll find out if he's about to lose his job. Then I wondered if this was a good time to bring up the pirate ghost and his idea of wanting me to help him find his gold. Next I thought about my becoming a Trojan horse and how delivering the last poster brought me face to face with Solo Yerkos.

But I still hadn't said a word, and I noticed Dark Cloud had turned his head slightly, cocking it away and not looking directly at me, the same way Solo Yerkos had viewed me at an angle. A strange vibration flowed through my body like an electric current shaking up my entire system. Maybe I'm getting a touch of the flu bug, I thought, and then I told myself, say something, dummy, he doesn't have all day.

Dark Cloud held up his hand. "It is true," he said slowly. "There is a bad spirit near you, an evil shadow. We must pray, my son. The Great Spirit will speak."

A cold shiver ran up my back. I really didn't want to hear too much about a bad spirit and an evil shadow, not if they were after me.

He heaved himself up to his feet, towering over us like a giant oak. He was about six foot six and twice as wide as any normal-sized man. He turned to the door of his cottage and went inside. I looked at George uncertainly.

"What happens now? Are we supposed to follow him?"

"I don't know," George said. "Better sit tight for a while. The main point is, I think he'll do the thing for you."

I wagged my head, stunned. "You know, he read every single thing in my head then. It was like he gave me a silent order to tell him what was bothering me, and I was thinking of how to tell him, only I couldn't say anything. But you heard what he said. He knew."

George shrugged, equally puzzled. "What was that thing about a bad spirit near you? How does he know that?"

"It's Shinnecock tribal magic, George. Stick around and learn something."

The door opened and Dark Cloud shuffled out holding some things in his hands. George bent close to whisper to me. "He's got the wampum belt. That's for ceremonies. The other thing is his deerskin spirit bag."

"He's got the Great Spirit in there?"

"No, man. It's his medicine bag, with his stuff in it for calling the Great Spirit. Be cool, man. He's going to say a prayer for you. Don't talk. Don't move a muscle. Sit quiet like a rock."

The massive shaman stood erect, facing the pale midday sun. He was humming a singsong chant under his breath, muttering strange-sounding words. Then he sank to his knees. With his finger he traced a circle on the hard earth. His chanting continued, sounding up from deep in his chest, strange singsong words. I looked at George and he shook his head as if telling me he didn't know the Shinnecock language either.

Dark Cloud picked some leaves from a yellowed hazel bush. Then he rooted around and found some small dried twigs. He mixed these together into a small pile. Sitting cross-legged, eyes closed, weather-beaten face lifted to the sky, he continued his soft musical chant.

He put his hands together, bowed his head, and was silent. Then he opened the deerskin pouch laced with leather drawstrings. He took out blue and white beads, colored stones and crystals, some feathers and small dried bleached bones. He placed these in a circle around the pile of twigs and leaves.

I began feeling nervous. I looked up and saw a small cloud forming in the clear sky. It moved quickly and blotted the sun. I looked at George, nodding my head upward. He followed my gaze and shrugged, his eyes blank.

Dark Cloud moved faster. He took two white beads and with a dark root, blackened one. He placed the white bead between my right thumb and index finger, and the black between my left thumb and finger. He pressed my fingers tightly together, illustrating with his own what I was to do. The strength and weight of his fingers as he pressed mine was another new experience for me. They could have been steel pliers.

I held my fingers together tightly. The small dark cloud still hung in the sky, not moving, covering the sun. I shivered.

Dark Cloud was swaying back and forth, singing softly in a mournful chant. Then he struck a match and dropped it on the small pile of leaves and twigs. A flame flickered in the center, and he sprinkled some reddish powder over it. The flame shot up suddenly, a foot high.

Dark Cloud raised his thick finger in front of my eyes commandingly. He pointed toward the leaping flame. "You look now," he said. "You look hard."

I stared obediently. The brilliant flame danced. The deep-voiced chant of Dark Cloud sounded again, the singsong tones rising, and falling to a whisper. Then he spoke.

"Great Spirit, I pray to you. Show the way. Dark Cloud is unworthy, Divine Father. His heart too heavy to trouble you. Now it is for my sons, my children, for the shadow that is over us. There is a hiding place where the Spirits do not see. It is in the Nightland, Great Father. Show us in the sacred fire what will be."

The flames crackled and my face felt the intense heat. I kept staring at the blaze, my fingers clenched tightly around the little beads Dark Cloud had placed there. Suddenly my left hand began to shake. The blackened bead he had placed there was moving. I tightened my grip but it continued to squirm between my fingers as if it was alive.

My left hand trembled and shook more violently.

Sweat dripped on my face as I gripped harder on the bead. I looked at Dark Cloud and he pointed impassively, directing my attention again to the fire. I stared at it, watching the flame dance. Smoke swirled darkly and the flame parted. My eyes bugged out and I heard George Cooper gasp. An indistinct swirling image was forming in the flame.

Suddenly it was a recognizable face and I stared at it, shocked and frightened. Solo Yerkos, thin lips twisted into a sardonic smile, looked up at me. The bead in my left hand shook as if struggling to get out. I bit my lip, holding on tight, wondering what was happening. The deep notes of Dark Cloud's song sounded louder.

Wondering if Dark Cloud had seen it too, I jerked my eyes from the twisting image of Solo Yerkos in the fire. He sat quietly, still chanting, gazing into the fire, his hooded eyes half-closed. Then he raised his thick arms to the sky. "Great Spirit, we thank you with loving hearts."

Singing softly now, he sprinkled a musk-scented powder over the flames. Slowly they died. A hissing sound came from the hot glowing ashes, and as I stared, the cruel smiling face of Solo Yerkos dissolved and vanished in swirling smoke.

"Open your hands, my son."

I opened my right hand. The white bead was there and Dark Cloud removed it. He tapped my tightly clenched left hand. I opened it slowly. The black bead was gone!

Afraid I had dropped it, I looked on the ground. "No," Dark Cloud said. "It is gone with the evil one."

I looked at my fingers. They were stained a dark color, as if the bead had dissolved. "Did you see him?" I said to Dark Cloud. "That's the man. His name is—"

Dark Cloud slowly shook his head. "It has no name, that one. It is the Nameless One who lives in the fire."

I remembered what Herky said. The odd chance of Solo Yerkos being the Devil because he had picked the Old King Dick house to live in. Was Dark Cloud telling me the same thing?

His heavy hand rested on my shoulder. His gray eyes were steady on mine. "The Great Spirit has spoken, my son. The test is yet to come. Your own spirit will tell you how to stand in the path of the fire that devours all."

My legs were wobbly when I got up. I wondered how to tell the old giant that my spirit felt weak and chicken, and was afraid of fire. I looked over at George. He was shaking his head, awed, still staring at the scorched ground.

Dark Cloud took my hand and pressed something soft into it. "Your heart will listen to the whispering wind of the Great Spirit," he said. "Use this, my son, when you hear the wind speaking to you."

I looked down at my hand. Dark Cloud had given me his sacred spirit bag.

George stood shyly looking up at the powerful old shaman. "I can't thank you enough, Great-grandfather, for this favor."

Dark Cloud nodded gravely. "You will tell your father Angry Runner that his son pleases me. You will also tell him you have been close to the Great Spirit."

He didn't tell us to leave but we found ourselves moving away. When we looked back, Dark Cloud was sitting exactly as we had found him, his eyes squinted against the sun.

The cloud was gone. The sky was clear.

"Hey, George," I said. "I want to thank you."

"Are you kidding, man? I want to thank *you*. That was an experience!"

"Too bad Herky couldn't come. With all he knows about facts, he would have flipped seeing something supernatural like that."

George nodded. "Well, I guess you won't leave out any of the details when you see him. And incidentally, that face in the fire, that Dark Cloud called the Evil One, the Nameless One. What's going on between you and him?"

I shook my head. "I don't know yet, George. Like Dark Cloud said, my test is yet to come."

"Yeah, man, I heard that. But who is he?"

"Solo Yerkos, the psychic I told you about before."

George nodded. "He looked mean enough to bite nails." He pointed to the deerskin pouch in my hand. "But don't forget to use Dark Cloud's spirit bag, if you have to. It may save your life."

I lifted the pouch. It felt awfully light. "You really think it will work?"

George smiled. "I can't wait until you tell me about it later."

I hoped he was right about that.

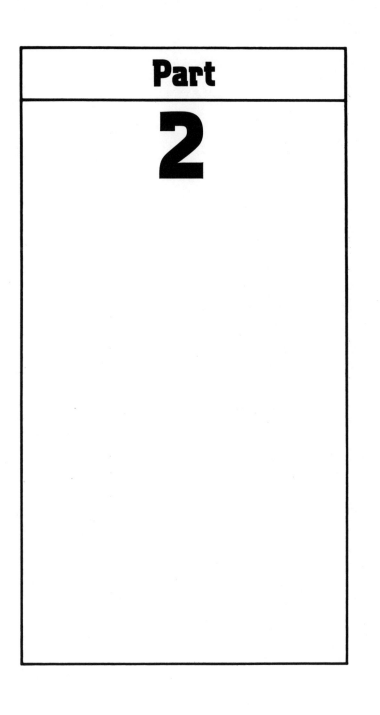

Part

2

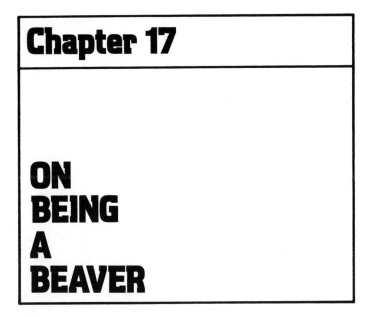

Chapter 17

ON BEING A BEAVER

After I got back, there was work to do around our house. The giant oak outside the front lawn had dropped about a million leaves to the wind. I had to rake and gather them into piles, then bundle them into bags for disposal.

Mom's flower beds were clogged with more leaves, the flagstones had drifted out of line, and part of the split-rail fence bordering our property had fallen and needed to be set in place again. I was so busy with the yardwork I didn't have time to review the day's activities with Sinbad.

When I was done, I dragged myself upstairs to wash for dinner. Sinbad came clattering up the steps behind me. "Later," I told him, "after dinner." He looked up at me with his dark scowl. "I don't think you'll believe what happened anyway," I told him. "I had some Indian magic. I can hardly believe it happened myself."

He looked awfully sad and disappointed so I showed him the spirit bag Dark Cloud had given me. "That's a real Shinnecock medicine bag," I told him. "Go ahead and laugh."

I held it out for him to sniff and he got all excited wanting to see what was inside. "Nothing doing," I said. "That's sacred spirit stuff. No dogs allowed."

Sinbad cocked his head and whined. He scratched at the wood floor with his big paws. He was definitely interested. He had probably scented the old bones Dark Cloud had inside.

"I'll tell you about it after we eat," I said, and put the spirit bag up on my highboy dresser where he couldn't get at it.

He followed me downstairs with a happy rush, losing his balance near the bottom as usual because of his momentum, and skidded with a crash into the front door.

"Nice going," I told him. "If you tried that out at the Old King Dick house, you'd probably knock the whole place down."

I shouldn't have brought that up, because I was trying to forget the scary vision of Solo Yerkos grinning up at me from the fire Dark Cloud had made. Luckily I've got a good appetite and recovered in time to put two hamburgers away, plus a pot of spaghetti and two glasses of milk with some apple pie.

Mom's used to my appetite and didn't say anything about me eating her out of house and home. I helped her with the dishes and cleaning up.

"When's Pop coming home?" I said.

She turned. "Pop? Your father? Do you really have a father? He's away so much, I hardly remember him. What was he like?"

The telephone rang. She picked it up and listened. "You must have the wrong number," she said. "There's only me here, and a fat dog, and a boy who can't remember what his father looks like."

"Ask him when he's coming home," I yelled.

"Ask who?" Mom said. "I don't know this man. He's a stranger. He lives in other people's houses."

She listened for a while longer, then hung up. "He said two more days. Whatever that means. Whoever he is."

That's Mom's way of coping with my pop being out so much of the time with these odd jobs fixing up old houses. We both missed him more than we let on. Sinbad, too, naturally.

Pop had a good attitude about things. He called it flowing with the current, not fighting it, going with life. He didn't hassle or worry about anything. "All the good things I've found have been mostly accidental," he once told me. "The bad things are going to happen anyway. So why not just go along with the current? Enjoy the scenery and the ride."

The way I was doing things, it now occurred to me, was counter to his theory. I seemed to be going off in all directions jumping from one thing to another, not really knowing where I was before I got to someplace else.

If Pop were with me now, I thought, he would be saying, "Not efficient. You're only borrowing trouble working against the grain. Be like the beaver. Simplify your life."

We'd been through it before. The beaver stayed with what he knew. He found a tree, cut it down, dragged it to the water, built his dam. You didn't see him running around chasing foxes, or arguing with birds. He did his job, period, like nature intended.

Upstairs, I grabbed Sinbad's thick neck and yanked him close. "We got to do it right from here on," I told him. "We got Dark Cloud's magic to help us if we get in a jam. Now what we have to do is just take care of one thing at a time. Then get on to the next."

Sinbad agreed, planting a wet slobbering kiss on my face. "I love you, too," I said, "but we got to start making some sense out of all that's happening, or admit we don't know what we're doing and quit the case."

Sinbad stretched out and looked up at me over his paws. "Okay," I said. "One thing at a time. We start with Gunther Waldorf. Either he's missing or he's not. I think last time with Sheriff Landry along, he faked me out. This time we got to come back with some real evidence. Okay? Let's go."

I got my squall coat and went downstairs again with Sinbad clumping along behind me. He waited until I found the book I wanted, high on the wall shelves my pop had built. I showed it to him. "If we're wrong, we're wrong, okay? Let's go."

I told my mom I was taking Sinbad out for a walk. At the door I slipped the thick chain leash on Sinbad. "All I want to do is ask him a few questions. You'll be there to back me up in case he gets mad."

Sinbad got the idea how important this mission was, and he chugged up our hill to Steamboat Road like an army tank without stopping once to chase any stray scents in the air. I had to run to keep up with him.

It was cool and quiet. No cars around. We got to the Waldorf driveway and I checked inside. Nobody there waiting to zoom out at us. The old house looked peaceful and beautiful in its setting among the pines. Smoke curled from the end chimney.

I knocked on the door using the heavy old brass ornament. I saw a curtain moving at the side bay window. Then the fan light went on and the door opened. He stood there tall and slender with the same kind of button-down old sweater the real Gunther Waldorf used to wear. He was smoking a pipe just like the real Gunther Waldorf, and he looked so much like the man he was supposed to be that for a moment I had to think I was crazy.

"Hi, Mr. Waldorf," I said cheerfully. "I was here the other night with Sheriff Landry, remember?"

He stared down at me coldly but then I saw a flicker of recognition in his spectacled eyes, pale blue just like you-know-whose. He nodded shortly. "Oh, yes. I signed the book, yes."

I pulled out my own book. "Right, for his daughter

Minerva. I didn't have mine along then so I brought it now. My English report has to be on ecology and I'm using your book on it. Would you autograph it, too, please?"

He smiled thinly, pulled a pen from his shirt pocket, and propped the book against the doorjamb. "Yes, of course. Your name, please."

"Steve Forrester. I used to deliver your newspaper a few years ago. I guess I never told you my name. Also I grew a lot and put on all this weight."

He was writing inside the book jacket, and stopped to stare at me. Then he smiled, nodding. "Oh, yes, of course. Very forgetful of me."

Sinbad at my knee whined. The man looked down and drew back a little, as people usually do when they first see my ferocious-looking monster. "This is my English bulldog Sinbad," I told him. "He used to come along sometimes. I think he still remembers you."

Sinbad, looking up with his crooked grin, cocked his head, and made the cracked-voice parrot sound. He wagged his tail, too, and it relaxed the man. I made a mental note to give him an extra-big dog biscuit for such good acting.

"Oh, yes," the man said. "Fine-looking animal." He leaned down to pat Sinbad's bulky shoulder. I saw dark roots under his silvery-gray hair.

He handed me the book. "There you are, Steve. I hope you will remember what is in it and get yourself good marks on your book report."

"Thanks a lot," I said. "I'll still have to read your other ones. This was your first on the ecology here and you didn't mention the Shinnecock Indians."

He blinked. "I didn't?"

"No, although I think you got to it in your later ones."

"Yes," he said slowly drawing on his pipe.

"And because right now our class is concerned with environment impact and depletion of our natural resources, I wondered if you were doing any new studies, like, you know, what happens if they discover oil on the reservation land."

He stared down at me. He relit his pipe. "Oil," he said. "Well, that is always a tricky question. You mean who is to get it—the Indians or the state?"

"Yeah, something like that."

He hesitated, frowning. "I think that is a political question, no? I write only about the conditions."

"Well, that's what I mean—I thought maybe you had some reports on the latest tests, so I could scoop my class."

He shook his head, smiling again. "I'm very sorry about that. I am still gathering information. My studies are not yet finished. So regretfully, I cannot help you there."

He half-bowed stiffly from the waist and was backing inside to close his door, when I added, "How's the narcissus and the tulips coming? I remember you were always working on them so you could have flowers in the fall."

"Oh," he said with a regretful shrug, "I'm afraid I have not had the time lately. Too much writing to do. So many books—"

"Too bad," I said. "They sure would have brightened your flower beds now."

He nodded and was closing the door. "Well, perhaps next year."

I waved the book. "Thanks a lot for your autograph, Mr. Waldorf. It was great talking to you."

"You are welcome, young man," he said, and the door closed.

Sinbad looked up at me and I snapped the chain. "Okay, wasn't that nice of him? Now let's go home and study."

We went down the long gravel path and nobody came running to capture us and torture us into revealing our mission and who sent us.

When we got past the gatepost and turned on to Steamboat Road, I congratulated Sinbad. "That was really terrific, the way you put on that friendly act. But you were there—you heard it all. If he was really Gunther Waldorf, he would know narcissus and tulips are spring flowers, not fall. He fell for that one, all right. Remind me, I owe you a big dog biscuit."

Sinbad grinned. He loves those big biscuits.

Chapter 18

POINTS ABOUT THE HAMPTON MYSTERY

Sinbad didn't let me forget my promise, and he attacked the giant dog biscuit I gave him with awesome crunches of his powerful jaws. I waited until he was finished before calling another meeting.

I placed the Gunther Waldorf book on the floor between us. It was titled: *Hampton: A Study in Local Ecology*. It was dated ten years earlier.

"Okay," I said, "The meeting is now open. Did we prove something or not? You don't have to give an opinion until I add it all up, okay?"

Sinbad nodded, stretched out in his favorite flying squirrel pose. " Point One," I said. "I don't know if you noticed, but he had dark roots under his gray hair. That might prove he's a phony and dyed his hair to look like Gunther Waldorf, except for the fact that I don't remember if the real Gunther Waldorf had dark roots or not. So we don't count that one as admissible evidence."

Sinbad blinked. It was okay with him. "Point Two," I said. "I told him you used to come with me when we delivered the daily newspaper. That was a fib because we both know you didn't. But he pretended you did, and went along. So either he lied about the real facts or didn't remember. No real evidence."

Sinbad burped and yawned. "Okay, I'll hurry it up. Point Three. When I asked him the questions about the oil and the Shinnecocks, he didn't jump. He stayed cool and gave us a good answer. So whoever he is, he's no dummy, and the guys who picked him for this impostor job knew what they were doing. There's no evidence there about anything for our side.

"But we got him on Point Four—the one about the tulips and narcissus. The real Gunther Waldorf knew all about plants. The only question is, Has he got too absentminded to pay attention to conversation? Answer, I don't think so. He answered the rest fine. So we got the one big point on him—he doesn't know beans about flowers."

Sinbad thumped his tail weakly on the wood floor. His eyes closed briefly. "Okay," I said. "That's it for tonight. I'm entering it all in this book now, so next time we talk to Sheriff Landry, we'll have all our facts and evidence, and he won't be able to blow us down for lack of the same. I also got to tell him about that scratch in the Lincoln fender. The same on both cars."

Sinbad began snoring. I got the notebook open and

wrote on the top of the first page: *The Hampton Mystery.*

Underneath, marking the date, I wrote an account of what had happened this night with the man who was taking the place of Gunther Waldorf.

I looked at my watch. There was still time for another checkout for evidence. Mrs. Teska never went to bed early.

I left Sinbad sound asleep, sneaked downstairs and told Mom where I was going, and ran up the hill. It felt good acting like a beaver, I thought. One thing at a time and do it right.

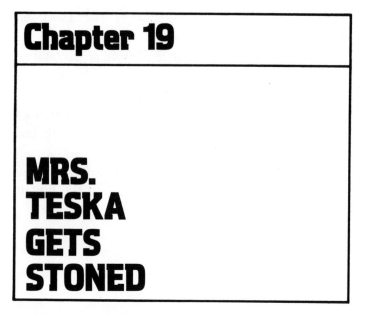

Chapter 19

MRS. TESKA GETS STONED

There were lights on in her rooms over the store, and I went up the stone side-steps and knocked. I heard her coming slowly toward the door. She peered out at me, surprised. "Is something be wrong, Stevie? You mama forget to buy some things? Wait, I go down and open store for you."

I told her no, it wasn't that, but I wanted to talk to her. She looked puzzled but shrugged her thick shoulders. "Hokay, so come inside. It be too cold out."

Her apartment was clean and tidy, as usual. There wasn't much furniture, only a few pieces. A china cabinet, a table, two chairs, her rocker. Small pictures of landscapes were on the walls, and the wood floor was partly covered with scatter rugs.

She offered me a chair and sat herself on her rocker.

"Is something important come up, Stevie? What for you here now? Is more news about election for sheriff?"

"No, Mrs. Teska. I've been doing a lot of thinking since last time. Mostly about this Solo Yerkos guy, that medium you found in town. Maybe you ought to speak to the lawyer Mr. Pickering before you go there again. You have a lot of money, you know. You were talking about giving everything up when you got ready, and so on. You're not some poor old immigrant lady now, Mrs. Teska. You're rich, you know."

She smiled. "Sure I know. Big Murdock was good mans. He give his Anna so much last time. Too much for this old woman."

"Well, that's great," I said. "But you know, sometimes people take advantage of old women with a lot of money, in this country. Like they promise them a lot of things, sell them phony gold mines, and so forth. So you have to be extra careful what you do with it."

She nodded. "Is why I go see this nice good man Solo Yerkos. Man with big heart like him, man who spirits trust. I know man like this okay for Mrs. Teska to trust also."

"But, gee, Mrs. Teska—holy smoke, what if—"

She held out her hand and took mine. "Is no worry for you, Stevie. Old peoples must do own way. Now Mrs. Teska listen to sister Sofi, and she tell true things, also."

I didn't know what to say. "But what if your sister—" I couldn't say more because how could I knock her sister in case it really was her spirit talking? "Well, okay," I said. "As long as you're real careful about things. I mean, like there's no hurry, is there?"

Mrs. Teska shrugged and patted my shoulder. A mischievous glint appeared in her eyes. "No, Stevie. No hurry now. Everything taken care."

"What does that mean?"

She smiled and walked to the china cabinet. "I show you, Stevie."

She opened a drawer, and came back holding a large flat manila envelope. She handed it to me, saying, "Here. You open and see how you like."

I undid the metal clasps and opened the flap. A small glossy photo slipped into my hand. I stared at it, not understanding at first. "What's this? It looks like a tombstone."

She nodded, smiling. "Is good black granite. You read what it says. Spelling is okay, Stevie?"

Letters were cut into the dark shining stone. They read:

HERE LIES
ANNA MYSZKA MURDOCK TESKA
80 years old

My hand shook. I heard her voice, sounding far away, asking how I liked it. I couldn't answer, my eyes riveted on the inscription. I knew Mrs. Teska had passed her eightieth birthday. She would be eighty-one at Christmas. It looked as if she had decided to die before.

"How do I like it?" I said dazed. "Well, it's real nice, Mrs. Teska. But how come you ordered it now?

Also what makes you so sure you're going to die soon? You're not sick, or even too old."

She shrugged. "No, but is always good idea for to be ready, I think. I know sister Sofi is waiting. So I have stone cut and made ready in time. Is very pretty stone. I like."

"How about your coffin?" I said, kidding. "You going to order that in advance, too?"

She pointed toward the curtained-off inner room. "I have already. Is in there. Very beautiful one. You want see?"

"No, thanks," I said, startled. "I'll take your word for it." I kept shaking my head, feeling dazed about all this. "Wow! I don't get it. What's the big rush?"

She rocked in her old chair. "Well, Stevie, you know Mrs. Teska no have any family to take care. So now when she die, she be no trouble to you, your mother, father. Everything is pay for now. Stone, coffin, cemetery. Only cost"—she took a folded slip of paper from her skirt pocket—"is cost seven thousand, five hundred dollars, all together. Is good fair price, you think?"

"Gee, I don't know about that stuff. Mrs. Teska," I said. "The thing that bothers me the most, I guess, is seeing that number on it—eighty—when you think you'll die. It's only a few months till the end of the year and your next birthday. Nobody knows exactly when they're going to die. I mean, especially when they're in good health like you are. It's—it's crazy."

She shrugged. "Sofi say for to be ready soon. So I get ready now."

She replaced the picture and set it back in the china-cabinet drawer. "Tomorrow, Stevie, Mrs. Teska find out for sure when is time to die."

"What do you mean, you're finding out tomorrow? Are you going to see a doctor?"

She pulled her red shawl around her shoulders. "No, no see doctor. I go see Solo Yerkos man for maybe last time. He say sister Sofi will come to say for sure, when we meet again. Spirits know for certain when it right time for to die, Stevie."

I couldn't believe all this but she looked serious. "What time are you going over to see Mr. Yerkos?"

She glanced at her wall clock. "Tomorrow night. Near eight o'clock. I take taxi so is nothing for to worry."

"Well, good luck," I said. "But maybe Sofi won't come. Or there's a chance she'll tell you not to do anything drastic yet. Maybe it will be postponed to a later date, Mrs. Teska."

She smiled. "Good night, Stevie boy. You go home and do more homework."

She was rocking in her chair when I left, not looking worried. I was doing enough of that for us both.

Chapter 20

CONTRACT WITH A GHOST

Sinbad opened one eye when I got into bed. "We got a tough situation there," I told him. "You'll never believe this, but Mrs. Teska is so ready to die, she already ordered her tombstone and coffin." He waited for my idea of how we would stop her or change her mind. But I didn't have any. He sighed and leaned on me, and soon fell asleep. In a little while I gave up worrying about it, and joined him in dreamland.

I dreamed that I was inside a real Trojan horse, only this time the city of Troy belonged to Solo Yerkos. My secret army had goofed off, and he knew where I was and began shooting laser beams from his eyes at me. They were zipping through the wood horse coming closer and closer when I heard Sinbad barking, as if he had come to my rescue. I told him to watch out for those laser beams but he only woofed as if he didn't believe me. I tried to grab him but he wouldn't stay still. He woofed again in my ear and I woke up. The ghost was at the foot of the bed again. I checked the clock on my dresser. After midnight.

He didn't waste time getting to the point. "I've given ye a few days, lad. Had any luck yet with me gold?"

"Hey, listen," I said, "I'm sorry but I've been too busy. A lot of other problems that I can't solve are bugging me, and I just haven't had time yet to get around to yours."

His luminous form wavered and seemed to float away. Then he got it all back together again, and drew himself up to his full height. "You'd not be denyin' a ghost a favor, matie? Not many'd be that wicked. After me last visit, I took it like a contract between us here. That ye'd be out diggin' for me gold what that Captain Bones, blast his sotted soul, done me out of." He waved one arm toward the window. "There's the beach yonder and the cave somewhere about. It needs yer doin', lad, an' make no mistake about it."

I shook my head, hoping he would be reasonable, and try to understand. "I'd really like to, Mr. Marion, but—"

His hazy form flared. "It's Captain Marion, if ye please. I had me own ship once, the *Unicorn*, but then the wind blew us ashore off them islands, an' the rocks did us in. It was after that, with no ship o' me own, I signed up with skipper Jack Bones, only t'get off the island, y'understand—"

His voice failed then, and I went on with my side

of it. "The trouble is the woman who owns all that beach property is a good friend of mine. And unless I can find a way to stop her, she's going to give it all away to a bunch of crooks." Sinbad woofed then and sat down, as if telling the ghost I wasn't kidding. "Tomorrow night," I added quickly.

His voice quavered. "What's that ye say? Givin' away me gold? I knew it! It's them vibrations what's got me all stirred up! There's been all that talk of gold an' the like. There's evil afoot there on the beach, I been thinkin'."

"Well, I don't know about that. She's a nice old lady." I decided to tell the whole story. The ghost listened. At times he faded away, and then came back to view. "Got to find a way to ration the energy, lad," he said hoarsely.

When I finished, he looked balefully at me with his one good eye. "The spirit of her sister, yer sayin'?"

"Yeah, that's what she thinks. But what if it's a fake? Somebody only pretending to be one."

He thought about it, very agitated, striding back and forth, waving his arms. I wanted to warn him about blowing his energy, but still didn't know him that well.

"I don't know what ye mean, lad. A spirit is a spirit, ain't it? Like me here now—I'm a proper one, ain't I?"

I nodded. "Sure you are. But what if this is all just a racket? A trick to make her think it's her sister's spirit?"

"Well, lad, it'll be easy enough to find out, won't it? Ye'll be tellin' me now where at all this is goin' to happen."

"It's the Old King Dick house down near the cove,

on Hellsfire Street. The red Garrison Colonial on the bluff right above the beach. Near where you think your gold is buried."

"No problem, matie. I'm thinkin' as how I know the place. Just tell me the time it's all to be happenin', an' I'll do me best to be there."

"Eight o'clock tomorrow night," I said. "I'll make a deal with you, Captain Marion. You help me with Mrs. Teska to make sure they don't cheat her or take her life, and I promise to do whatever you say. I'll spend the rest of my life looking for your gold."

The ghostly figure swelled briefly. "Aye, laddie, it's a solid contract we're havin'. I'll do me best if the energy permits, and then give you a chance to be at yer own word."

He began to fade fast, and with his last words he was gone as suddenly as he had appeared. I grabbed Sinbad around his thick chest and held him tightly.

"Did you hear all that?" I told him. "The ghost is going to help us take care of Mrs. Teska. How about that?"

Sinbad kept staring into space, his muzzle pointing where the ghost had been. He whined softly, looking sad and disappointed.

"It's the energy," I said. "He likes you but he just can't stick around too long."

Sinbad turned his head quickly and gave me a slobbering kiss. He put his heavy head on my chest and lay down again. His ears fluttered, and in a little while he was snoring.

"That's okay," I told him. "Pleasant dreams."

Chapter 21

THE GREAT GARBAGE CAN CAPER

My mom was cheerful at breakfast Sunday morning. "While you and your fat friend have been sleeping, I've been busy on the phone with a strange man who claims to be your father and my husband. He's invited me to spend the rest of the weekend with him out at Montauk."

"But it's already Sunday," I said. "Pop knows you got to be at work Monday and—"

Mom dropped some more pancakes on my plate. "Not this Monday. Don't you keep up with current events? This Monday is Columbus Day, a legal holiday, in honor of the great navigator who freed the slaves."

"That was Lincoln," I said.

"I'm talking about us working slaves," Mom said. "Anyway, I decided to accept his offer as I might not ever see him again in this lifetime. I'm afraid your father is hooked on his filthy habit of restoring old houses, and will always be away. Did I hear you say you and Sinbad are perfectly capable of looking after each other today and tomorrow?"

"No problem," I said. "Have a good time. Is there food?"

Mom opened the fridge and pointed. "There's always food, but with you two who can say it will ever be enough?"

"Okay," I said, "we'll make it last. And if it doesn't, Mrs. Teska has enough tuna and peanut butter and milk and dog food to keep us going."

"Good boy. Then I'll be off as soon as I throw a few sexy things together."

She went upstairs, came down in a little while, and hugged me good-bye. She stooped over and rumpled Sinbad's skin. "You take care of each other now," she said, and Sinbad rolled around on the floor groaning in ecstasy. I guess he really loves Mom best.

She went out the front door, got into the car, and was off in a fast start up our hill. I had to hold Sinbad around his thick neck and shoulders with all my might or he would have gone right through the picture window after her.

"Relax," I told him. "She's gonna see Pop. It's only for a few days."

Sinbad stared out the window longingly until the sound of the engine died, and then he licked my face to let me know he was okay now. "Good deal," I said. "Now we got to get organized about tonight."

I knew there was nothing I could do about it if Mrs. Teska decided to give all her money away. I didn't like the idea of her dying right away just because her sister Sofi's spirit told her to. But there was a chance I could see for myself just what kind of spirit her sister Sofi was.

The phone rang. It was Minerva.

"If I didn't know you any better," she said, "this time I might think you were right."

"About what, Minerva?"

"About Gunther Waldorf being kidnapped."

I looked at Sinbad. "It's Minerva. She knows something we don't know." He wagged his tail happily at her name.

"I guess now you're stumped wondering how I know," she said.

"I don't even know *what* you know, Minerva."

"I'm telling you," she said. "I know he was kidnapped."

"Okay," I said cautiously, "only what made you change your mind, all of a sudden?"

"It wasn't all of a sudden," she said. "It took time because first I had to read all his books, and then I had to check his garbage can."

"You what?"

"Well, let's start with the man who is pretending he is Gunther Waldorf, and fooling a lot of people, including my pop. Now if he was the real Gunther Waldorf, he would still be eating the same things, wouldn't he? I mean, he wouldn't suddenly be changing his eating habits?"

"That's a good point, Minerva."

"The trouble with you is you never document your facts. For example, you were right there when you saw the man being kidnapped, but you never thought of proving he wasn't there."

"Well," I said, "I'm still working on that."

"Save your breath," she said. "I've already proved it."

"Like how?" I asked.

"I told you. By reading his books and checking his garbage cans." She waited but I refused to bite, and she got on again. "Well, if you had read his books, you would know Gunther Waldorf is a strict vegetarian. He writes about all the wild plants he knows how to eat, how he could eat his way across a country ditch, and so on."

"I think she's got something," I told Sinbad. "Okay," I said to Minerva, "and what's in the garbage cans?"

"Lots of bones," she said. "Meat and chicken bones. Also empty bottles of booze. Gunther Waldorf never drank."

"How do you know that?"

"It's in his books, too. No smoking, no drinking, eating only natural foods, no meat."

"That's it? That's your proof?"

"Well, of course not," she said. "I don't go off half-baked, like you do. I had brains enough to check with Sidney Beller, the market delivery boy."

"On what he used to deliver to Gunther Waldorf and what he delivers now?"

"Right on," she said. "And it's all changed, he said, dating practically to the very night you thought you saw something funny going on."

"I didn't just think so, Minerva. I knew I saw it. Only when your pop came down with me, this new Waldorf looked and sounded so much like the old one, he faked me out. And your old man chewed me out later for jumping to conclusions."

"Well, frankly," she said, "I had to agree with him. You sounded like a real nut."

"Okay. So have you told him what you found out?"

"No way," she said. "The only thing my pop understands or recognizes is real proof. Can you see me going to him with my story of the bones and bottles in the garbage cans?"

"It sure sounds like reliable evidence to me, but your old man is kind of stubborn, Minerva."

"It's no problem. All we have to do is follow up on this and find the real Gunther Waldorf. The one you saw driven off without his overcoat."

"What if we can't find him?" I said.

"Don't worry, we will."

"That's okay with me. Then I can concentrate on Mrs. Teska, and find a way to keep her from handing over her money and getting ready to die."

"I know you've been working on that. How you doing on it?"

"It depends on what happens tonight. She's going to Solo Yerkos's house to get the final instructions from her sister Sofi's spirit."

"No sense asking, but I suppose you'll be there, too, right?"

"Well, I got to find out if it's all on the level, don't I? If it's not a ripoff, I got to butt out of it, I guess. I'll tell you all about it tomorrow."

"You mean, if you live through it," she said. "Rotsa ruck."

I know Minerva's sense of humor, and I hoped she was kidding this time.

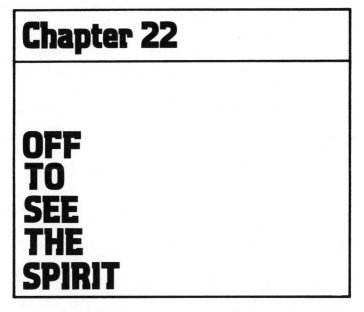

Chapter 22

OFF TO SEE THE SPIRIT

I had to get to the old Garrison Colonial before Mrs. Teska arrived for her seance with Solo Yerkos. There was still the problem of my finding a way inside first. It was night when I approached it.

The wind came up from the high bluff side of Jonah's Bay and I shivered. The pale-gold full moon gleamed over the darkening water. Small breakers ruffled the early evening tide, lapping at the sandy stretch of beach below. This was the area the ghost had told me about, where his gold was buried. I shook my head wondering how many more impossible things I had to try before things became normal again.

A giant elm across the street gave me a good hiding place until the shadows darkened on the Colonial grounds. Lights were on in the upper story, the lower floor still dark from the rear. Mid-front, the dining room area was dimly lit. I had come up from the bluff side and couldn't tell from my position if the tombstone lights were on yet over the front door.

Leaning my bike against the tree, I shifted the small cassette tape recorder from my cold stiff fingers to inside my squall coat. Herky had asked how I was going to get into the old house to record the seance. I reminded him about the secret exits and entrances these old houses had, for protection against witch-hunts or other attacks.

"I know you're an expert on old houses," he said. "But what if Solo Yerkos know about these secret passages, too? He might have them blocked up so that nobody can enter or leave."

"He might not know, Herk. Maybe he hasn't lived there that long. And in many cases, even the real estate people who handle the property don't know about them. I admit Yerkos can read minds, but maybe he can't read houses."

"It still sounds dangerous to me," Herky said. "If I'd known your plans, I could have rigged up an amplified mike bugging-device for you. You just stick it against the window, and we could pick it all up on tape a safe distance away. You might have been able to bug Mrs. Teska—drop it in her purse, even better."

"There wasn't time. I'm hoping my recorder will pick up the conversation when I get inside."

"It's possible, Steve, but you would have to get very close with your mike. That's what makes it so dangerous."

"Well, I got to try it, Herk. Maybe they'll all be so busy at the seance, they won't notice where I'm at."

"Where do you expect to be hiding—in the front parlor?"

"Don't be funny, Herk. Not in but under. There's usually a listening or prayer room in those old Colonials. All I got to do is find my way in, and work my way up."

"You're basing this whole adventure on your unproven theory that Yerkos is a fake and crook. What if her sister's spirit really appears, and tells Mrs. Teska she'll be dead soon and so she'd better sign away her money now?"

"It would be a blow, all right. But it's important to find out if she tells Mrs. Teska exactly how to get rid of her money. Whether to leave it to charity or Solo Yerkos. If I can get that on tape, I'll really have a good case against him."

Herky shook his head. "It's all too suppositional. And I'm convinced this is a job for Sheriff Landry or the D.A.'s office. The trouble is you're emotionally involved with Mrs. Teska, so you can't be objective. What did Dark Cloud tell you about this?"

"He only said I was up against this evil spirit, and it was going to be up to me and my own spirit."

Herky smiled. "That's interesting. In other words, Dark Cloud gave you an even chance. A one-on-one situation."

I thought about that now as the sky darkened, the shadows lengthened, and my watch told me it was time I got going before Mrs. Teska arrived. Crossing the street, I skirted the house to approach it from the rear bluff side. The wind blew hard as I leaned over the edge of the cliff. The beach was about fifty feet below. It was possible that somewhere along the cliffside, a secret tunnel had been cut out long ago leading to the house. There wasn't time now to check the hardened clay and fissures. If I did find a tunnel there, it was likely the walls had fallen after all the years, blocking any route through to the Garrison Colonial above.

A stand of straggly pines offered a windbreak at the rear close to the bluff. When some racing clouds passed across the moon, I ran between their shadows. Nearing the house, I bumped into something I didn't expect. It was a small old circular well, made of wood, with an A-shaped planked overhang. It seemed dumb to sink a well that far from the front of the house. In winter, by the time you got the water back to the kitchen, it could freeze to ice.

Ducking under the overhang, I could see the dark glitter of water. There were small stones on the ground and I tossed one down. *Plink!* The splash didn't sound right. I dropped another. *Plink!* The sound should have been a *thunk* or *plunk*.

I found a long windblown branch and dipped it down. When I held it up, the tip showed only a few inches of water. This had to be one of the weirdest wells ever dug because the bottom was at ground level!

You don't get a chance to find a fake well often, and the trick now was to move it. The idea was to get it tilted so that it could be rolled aside. Doing it took longer than getting the idea.

Underneath the false well-bottom was a thin cover of straw. Under that was sand and some gravel. After brushing away the ground cover, my hand hit a metal lid, it was about the size of a garbage can cover, but more important, it had to be the secret entrance to an underground passage!

The lid was iron and was heavy. I lifted it off and set it aside. I peered down a dark sewerlike opening. My flashlight revealed an iron-runged ladder under the rim, and after a deep breath, I climbed down.

My head was below the ground surface when I got my first negative feedback. The dry well was off its usual base now, the tunnel opening exposed with its lid off. Anybody patrolling the grounds might notice this, and if they didn't flush me out below, they might close the lid and put the well back to its former position, sealing me in.

I thought about it. You sure you don't mind getting sealed in, I asked myself. Finally I said forget it, it won't happen, come on, we're gonna be late for the seance.

That's my secret about how those big win-or-lose decisions are made, sometimes.

The tunnel's clay walls were shored up by heavy timber. It was dark, cold, and damp. The narrow beam of my flashlight picked up the path of the excavation, and I went along cautiously hoping I wouldn't run into any rats.

Whoever dug the tunnel had done a good job, knowing his life and that of his family depended on it. It was narrow, but the heavy timber shoring the sides and buttressing the ceiling looked solid enough to last forever. Another tunnel might have been dug, too, I thought, leading directly to the beach below the bluff for a fast getaway by boat.

The tunnel widened at the end near a chimney foundation. The wood-slatted door near it was mildewed, made of heavy planks. I tugged hard at its iron hinge and the old door creaked and opened.

The floor was of pinewood, the walls joined-wood planks. I flashed my light around. At the far end was a ladder under a small trapdoor. It could lead to the kitchen above, or to the rear keeping room, the old name for the front parlor.

This must have been the old prayer room, sometimes called the listening room. In the old days they did a lot of both, and sometimes it saved their lives.

My flash picked out relics of the past as I swept it around the room. A porcelain washbasin in the corner on the floor. Metal buckets, and some of wood, and chipped enamel jugs. An old grinder, a teakettle, a pile of rotted boots and shoes, a candle stuck in the bottom of a pewter cup. Rotted rags, sacks of dried-out grain and corn cobs. An iron bedstead with a thin mattress and ragged blanket.

A soft moaning sound came from across the room, and I nearly dropped my flash. Something stirred under the bed blanket. My heart thumped as I came closer.

It was a man, no ghost or skeleton. Old but not that old.

I touched his shoulder and his eyes opened behind steel-rimmed glasses. They stared up into my face without any recognition.

"How you doing, Mr. Waldorf?" I said.

Chapter 23

A CROOKED MEETING

Gunther Waldorf's lips moved. I bent closer but couldn't hear anything. His face was pale and there were beads of sweat on his forehead.

"Are you okay?" I said. "And anyway what are you doing here?"

His blue eyes stared vacantly upward without focusing. I put my flash closer and noticed his pupils were dilated. His breathing was shallow.

"It looks like they drugged you, Mr. Waldorf," I said. "But don't worry. I'll get you out of here. Only first I got to go up that ladder and check something. I'll be right back."

He showed no response to me or what I said. If he wasn't being held prisoner, I couldn't guess what he was doing there. No more than I could figure out what the man who looked enough like him to be his twin or double was doing in the Waldorf house.

I had told him I would get him out, but in his weakened condition, I couldn't guess how I was going to do that, either.

I wished Sheriff Landry was with me now so I could prove I wasn't crazy. But Gunther Waldorf didn't look able to run away, and I still had business upstairs with the tape recorder.

I climbed the ladder to the trapdoor in the ceiling and heard voices. I pushed it open a crack, hoping no one would notice, and then more by degrees.

I was early. Mrs. Teska hadn't arrived yet.

Four men were sitting twenty feet away at a Queen Anne rosewood table in the dining room. The trapdoor was in the front parlor, hidden from their view, under a small table.

Solo Yerkos sat at one end, Brad Case at the other. I recognized the two other men, too. The short chunky guy called Calloway. The big guy he had called Joe that time at the Citizens' Committee store headquarters.

Big Joe was speaking. "It's up to Calloway. We're all set to do the number on the Indians."

Brad Case leaned forward, waving his hands. "We may be moving too fast. What do you think, Mr. Calloway?"

I pressed the "record" button down on my cassette recorder and pushed it up close to the trapdoor opening. My plan had been to record Mrs. Teska's seance with Yerkos, but what was going on now seemed important, too. I never expected these guys.

Calloway puffed on a long cigar. "We can't hold Waldorf here forever. Simpson's getting nervous at the house, worried the butler suspects something is wrong. You don't step into somebody else's shoes that easily." He turned to Solo Yerkos. "Has Waldorf talked yet?"

Solo Yerkos looked uncomfortable, on the defensive. "I'm sorry, gentlemen, but so far, he has resisted hypnosis and the mind-control drugs. That private study he has made of the Shinnecock offshore and inland oil and mineral deposits remains his secret. He has a strong will, that man, and although his body has weakened, his mind is still stubbornly locked. I need more time."

Big Joe's fingers drummed on the table. "Okay, so Waldorf won't go along. The Shinnecock elders through their council won't permit any more geological studies of their land. But we can go in there by provoking an incident. With the public impatient for oil, we won't have any trouble getting inside there and doing our own report."

Calloway nodded, and looked at Brad Case. "That answer your question, Brad?"

I wished Mr. Gideon Pickering was able to hear what was going on now.

Brad Case looked pale and tired. "We still have a few weeks before the election. When do you propose to have this take place?"

Calloway screwed up his pudgy face. "Within the

week, I'd say, Brad. Give the voters something to get steamed up about. Nothing like giving them something to think about before they go to the polls. We show the natural resource is there, and being deliberately and systematically destroyed."

"How do you mean—destroyed?" Brad Case asked.

Calloway smiled knowingly. "We start a fire or two. That stuff will burn for days. It'll be a running disaster, reminding the people of Hampton that the officials they put into office last election are siding with the Indians, wasting our precious natural resources."

Brad Case leaned back, looking uncomfortable. "Not a bad idea, I suppose, if you think you can get away with it."

Calloway puffed on his cigar. "Leave it to me. Joe and I will work out the details."

Joe nodded. "We've got a man at the Bureau of Indian Affairs, Brad. He'll back us all the way. The Shinnecock don't own the land. The government's only leased it to them. If we want a little chunk back, we can get it."

Solo Yerkos interrupted, waving his pale hands. "It may still be unnecessary—if I can induce Gunther Waldorf to reveal his statistical study of the reservation land and offshore water."

Calloway stubbed his cigar out, frowning. "Well, maybe, and again maybe not. You've had him long enough. We'll give you till the middle of next week. If he doesn't break, we'll go ahead with the corporation plan to drill inside there. Waldorf is a prominent man, you know, and we can't take the chance of Simpson at the house giving it all away to some nosy reporter who might just come along."

Solo Yerkos spread his hands. "Waldorf may still break. In the meantime, there is the other matter. The other property you are interested in." He looked at his wristwatch. "Mrs. Teska should be arriving here in about fifteen minutes. I expect no difficulty in getting her to sign over her holdings."

Calloway moved his chair back and edged his bulk out of it. "Well, you get that one settled, Yerkos, and you'll have earned your fee. Call me later and we'll talk about it."

Joe leaned toward Solo Yerkos, his face tight and threatening. "This one is supposed to be right up your alley, Yerkos. Just a little superstitious old lady. Let's hope you can handle it."

Yerkos stared back at him unruffled. "I expect no problem here. I suggest you gentlemen leave now before she comes. And I'll get back to Waldorf as soon as possible."

Joe raised three fingers. "You've got three more days, Yerkos. That's it."

Calloway was putting on his hat, getting into his overcoat. He tapped the big guy's arm. "Let's go, Joe. We've got to meet now with the lawyers, and work this out without it backfiring."

Solo Yerkos showed them to the door. A cold blast of wind swept in when he opened it. They walked out single file with Brad Case last. He half-turned toward

Yerkos as the others went out the door. "We don't want Waldorf hurt, you know. Just loosen his tongue and his memory."

Yerkos nodded. "He may be ready later tonight. I'll work on him again."

The wind rattled the lamps. Brad Case lowered his head and hurried out the door. Solo Yerkos closed it behind him. For a moment his lean body sagged weakly back against the door. His face was pale and he looked troubled. I pressed the "stop" button on my cassette recorder, and ducked down, closing the trapdoor over my head.

I waited breathlessly a few seconds, hoping he wouldn't come down now after Mr. Waldorf. I heard his footsteps vibrate off to the other side of the house. Then I checked my watch with the flash. Mrs. Teska was due any minute.

So was her sister Sofi's spirit.

Chapter 24

THE MYSTERIOUS SPIRIT OF SISTER SOFI

The prayer room was cold. It was an unheated basement and I sat on the ladder rung under the trap door shivering. I wondered how Gunther Waldorf in his weakened and drugged condition was bearing the low temperature, and as if in answer to my thought, I heard him groan.

I flashed my light down to the corner and saw he had thrown off his blanket. I got down there and wrapped it around him again. He was still perspiring, his eyes closed, a thin trickle of saliva oozing from his lips. His forehead felt hot.

As I tucked the blanket corners under the mattress, his hand suddenly clutched my wrist. Although he was drugged and in bad shape, his grip was surprisingly strong. I nearly yelped. Don't be scared, I told myself.

I swung the light to his face, and his eyes opened. Again they stared at me without focus or recognition. "It's okay, Mr. Waldorf," I whispered. "I'm your friend. You'll be okay."

His cold blue eyes stared on mine. His lips moved, and he moaned softly. His eyes closed and his grip relaxed. I pried his fingers off, and went back up the ladder.

I heard a door slam, and footsteps. I carefully lifted the trapdoor again. Mrs. Teska had arrived.

Solo Yerkos was pulling out a chair for her at the short left side of the long Queen Anne table, and then he sat to her right at the center. Mrs. Teska was wearing her old red shawl, and I saw her in profile. Yerkos was directly facing me across the darkened front parlor, but I doubted that he could see the narrowly opened trapdoor at that distance.

There was a small lamp on the table between Yerkos and Mrs. Teska, and sconces on the wall. A light filmy curtain hung in the doorway across the room from Mrs. Teska. I hadn't noticed it before. Behind that curtain would probably be the staircase leading upstairs, a small maid's room or study, and the kitchen.

Yerkos had his eyes closed, and began breathing heavily, inhaling slowly. It looked like he was going into a trance. His long white fingers tapped the table-top, as he leaned back against the high red-tufted Jacobean chair. His voice was deep and sonorous. "We welcome all spirits. If there is a spirit present, speak, we pray you."

Mrs. Teska's eyes were fastened on the curtain, her

thick shoulders hunched forward. Now Yerkos began to breathe more slowly, as if asleep. His head drooped. Suddenly there was a light tinkling sound, like tiny glass pieces moved together by a breeze. Then I heard a high-pitched giggling sound, a girl laughing. I froze, feeling the hair in back of my head standing up.

"Sofi is here, Anna. Can you see me?"

It was the voice of a young girl, musical and cheerful. Mrs. Teska stared, her jaw open slackly. The curtain billowed.

"Sofi?" Mrs. Teska whispered hoarsely. "Is that you, sweetheart?" She stared hard at the curtain, leaning forward. "I no see you, I only hear."

"I am here with you, sister," the young girlish voice said. "I see you sitting there, Anna, wearing your red shawl and dark blouse. Can you see me now?"

I watched Solo Yerkos closely. His lips were parted and moving with each word, but he looked asleep. The girl's voice was coming from the other side of the room. Maybe he knew how to throw his voice.

Mrs. Teska shook her head. "No, Sofi. Anna no see. Where is for to look, sweetheart?"

"Over here," the childlike voice said. "Here, Anna."

The curtain billowed out again as if blown by a sharp gust of wind behind it. Suddenly I was sweating just like Mrs. Teska. In the center of the curtain, glowing now and flickering like a flame, was the ghostly shadow of a slender girl.

Mrs. Teska smiled, nodding her head happily. "Yes, Sofi, I see you now."

The curtain buckled and billowed back. The spectral

shape flickered, changing form, becoming larger and then smaller. A high keening sound came from the curtain, like a longdrawn sigh, as the image grew smaller and smaller, threatening to disappear. It reminded me of my pirate ghost and his own flickering form and complaint about losing his energy.

My ghost had been shadowy but had revealed his features. I didn't know him, had never heard of him, yet there hadn't been any doubt at all about his being a ghost. He not only spoke hollowly like one, he looked like one. A shadowy apparition with a distinct framework I could see through, luminous and not solid.

This flickering spirit was different, a shadowy outlined image, not as ghostly once the initial shock was over. I realized that Mrs. Teska had been living in my neighborhood for over fifty years, ever since she was a young girl in her teens named Anna Myszka. She had told me her sister Sofi had died in the old country when she was a young girl. So Mrs. Teska hadn't seen her sister for over sixty years, and now she recognized not only the voice but also the strange flickering form as Sofi's.

I felt like popping up out of the trapdoor opening and telling her, "Mrs. Teska, sixty years is a long time to remember anybody, even somebody you loved. Why don't you get up and take a good look around in case this is a big ripoff?"

But I didn't say anything and stayed where I was peeking out from under the trapdoor in the old parlor, hoping that my recorder was getting everything down on the tape. It would run forty-five minutes on each side.

Solo Yerkos sat swaying and shaking as if he was having a bad dream. "Speak, spirit," he said, in his deep resonant voice. "Do you have a message for any of us here from the other world?"

The flickering form was steadier now on the rippling curtain. The voice spoke. "Yes, a message for my dear sister Anna. I want her to come and join me. It is time for her to leave her world now."

Solo Yerkos jerked his head, his eyes still closed. "Do you hear, Mrs. Teska?" he droned sleepily. "The spirit has a message for you. Can you hear her?"

Mrs. Teska was smiling and crying at the same time. Her short husky arms stretched over the table toward the shadowy figure on the curtain. "Yes, I hear, Sofi. Anna ready. She go when you say. Today, tomorrow, is make no difference. You tell me when, sweetheart."

Solo Yerkos's head hit his chest. He jerked it up, again it sagged, and he made a snoring sound. It was a good performance.

The image swayed. "Tomorrow, Anna," the spirit voice said. "I can't wait much longer for you. Tomorrow night. Mama is here, too, Anna. She is also waiting. Tomorrow night you will see her, too, and papa."

Mrs. Teska's eyes were streaming tears. "Yes, I be ready tomorrow night, sweet Sofi girl."

Solo Yerkos jerked his head again. "Is there any other message, spirit? I feel something is not yet decided." He stretched his hands outward. "Nothing must be left undone, spirit, or this woman will be unhappy in the spirit world with you."

The tinkling sound came again, the curtain billowed out, and then the voice laughed lightly. "What is there to decide? Anna, you come as you are. You don't need anything. You can get rid of your belongings now, and live with us in peace, and want for nothing."

Mrs. Teska nodded. "Whatever you say, Sofi." She opened her handbag, dipped her hand inside, and brought out a checkbook. "So there is no more need for money, and so much property. But I not know who to give everything to."

She took out a pen and looked at Yerkos. He snored, eyes closed. There was a soft sighing sound from the curtain.

"You must do two things, Anna. You make out the check to the man Yerkos who has brought us together."

Mrs. Teska nodded, her pen over the checkbook. "Yes, I do that now, Sofi dear. To Mr. Yerkos. And what else I do?"

The spirit voice sounded warm and patient. "You write on the paper there, Anna. You sign over your property, whatever land you have. You won't need it anymore when you are with us. You won't need anything, dear sister."

Although Solo Yerkos seemed asleep, somehow he managed to move a sheet of paper closer to Mrs. Teska. She set it in front of her, her pen ready. "Yes, sweetheart, I do it now. I make this out to Mr. Yerkos, also?"

"Yes, Anna."

The room became so quiet I could hear Yerkos snoring and the scratching sound as Mrs. Teska's pen began writing on the paper. She said sharply, "Wait, put paper down, please. I not signed yet—"

I stared as the paper rose from the table, and floated

in midair. Solo Yerkos opened his eyes wide, blinking. The white paper floated in front of his face, and then a hand materialized, holding it.

A shadowy outline took shape slowly. It was familiar to me now, and ghost or not, I wanted to hug it.

The burly ghost towered over Yerkos. "Here, now, and what's all this?" Captain Marion roared. "She can't be givin' the property over to you—ye scalawag!"

Yerkos sat bolt upright. He tried to grab for the sheet of paper but the ghost jerked it out of his reach. "Avast there! She can't hand it over, ye landlubber," yelled the ghost, "because what's buried in there belongs to me, an' I'll not be cheated again o' what's rightful mine."

Solo Yerkos got to his feet. He fell across the table staring at the ghost. "What is this?" he said hoarsely. "Who are you?"

"A dead man, and that's for sure," the ghostly pirate said. "But she can't be givin' you what's mine, now can she?" He turned toward the shadowy image on the curtain. "And what's all this yer doin', pretendin' to be of the other world?"

As he came closer to the curtain waving his arms, there was a scream from behind it. The youthful figure grew small, and then vanished. I thought I heard running footsteps on the stairs.

Mrs. Teska sat shaking her head. "Sister, where are you?" she cried. "What happened?"

The ghost turned his wrathful face, his single eye glaring at Mrs. Teska. "It was never yours to give away in the first place," he roared. "The man who owned all this is dead a long time, too, and that was Captain Billy Murdock."

Mrs. Teska looked frightened. She crossed herself. "Murdock," she mumbled. "Yes, Murdock."

The ghost waved the paper in his hand. "And now it's down to a scrap of paper, is it? I'll have ye know there'll be no tamperin' with the rights to me gold."

He walked across the room, heading for me and my hiding place. I dropped the trapdoor quickly before Yerkos saw me.

It didn't stop the ghost. He flowed through the floor and materialized in the air floating beside me as I clutched the ladder. He pushed the piece of paper into my hand.

"There you are, matie," he said hoarsely. "You'll be holding onto this until the business is done. And you'll be getting on with the work proper, as we agreed."

I had forgotten our agreement, putting it aside and out of my mind as something too impossible to worry over. But the paper in my hand along with the spirit's retreat, was a solid reminder of the bargain set in my room at his last visit. He had kept his word, his end of it.

The ghost sighed and began to thin out before my eyes. I wanted to tell him to stick around for a while, there might still be trouble ahead.

His bulky form was a thin remnant now. "Aye, lad, it's the energy goin' again, blast it. I'll have to be leavin' ye now, and we'll meet up again when the task is done proper."

His final words were still in the air when he vanished.

I remembered Solo Yerkos starting forward after the ghost before I ducked down under the trapdoor. There wasn't time to listen closely to find out if he was coming down after me.

I hurtled down the ladder while I was still ahead, toward the door to the secret passageway.

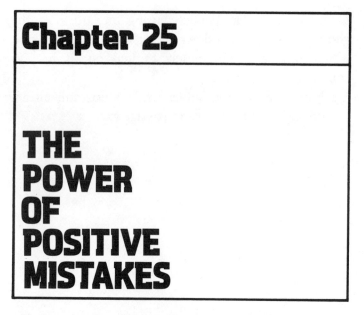

Chapter 25

THE POWER OF POSITIVE MISTAKES

Minerva Landry opened the door, looking surprised to see me. She was wearing white pajamas with red stripes. Her hair was in a ponytail. "Don't you know about bedtime?" she said.

"I found him," I yelled. "I was right! You were right! Is your dad home?"

She closed the door quickly against a whistling blast of cold night wind. "Sure he's home. He's in his den watching a fight on TV. Who did you find?"

"Gunther Waldorf," I said. "He's being held prisoner in the Old King Dick house. Solo Yerkos has him all drugged up and he can't talk. You better call your old man, Minerva. It could be a matter of life and death."

She looked me over calmly. "Well, I don't know.

Interrupting him when he's watching a fight can almost be a matter of life and death, too. Can't it wait a few more rounds?"

Sheriff Landry loomed in the doorway. "Can't what wait?" he barked.

Minerva shrugged. "Steve didn't know you were watching the fight, Pop. He found Gunther Waldorf. You know, the one you said wasn't kidnapped."

Sheriff Landry stared down at me. "What have you been up to this time?"

I held up the recorder. "Mrs. Teska was due over at Solo Yerkos's, that medium's place, tonight at eight o'clock. To find out from her sister's spirit whether she was supposed to die right away or not. Also she was going to give all her money and property away."

"Hardly your business," he said.

"Well, maybe," I said. "But I wanted to find out if she was going to give everything she owned to that Solo Yerkos guy. I always knew he was a phony." I waved the recorder. "You'll see. I got it all down here."

He ignored the recorder. "Something you were saying about finding Gunther Waldorf, I believe."

"That's right, Sheriff. I went in through a secret tunnel I found. It brought me right to the old prayer room—it's like a hidden basement of the house, you know—"

"Get to the point," he said coldly.

"Well, there he was—Gunther Waldorf—lying on a cot down there—and his eyes looked kind of funny, like he was drugged—and he didn't recognize me."

I waved the recorder again. "It's all down here. They

had this meeting. All these phony guys from the new Citizens' Committee—like Brad Case, and Calloway—"

"Who?" he said.

"Calloway. You know, that guy from the bank. And somebody called Joe. A big guy. And they asked Yerkos how he was doing with Waldorf because Simpson was getting worried and nervous—"

Sheriff Landry didn't change expression. "Simpson," he said.

"Yeah. He's the guy at Gunther Waldorf's house pretending he's the real Gunther Waldorf. Only he's not because the real one is down there in the prayer room. And then Solo Yerkos told everybody how he wasn't responding right yet to the hypnosis and the mind control drugs and—"

"You've got it all on that recorder?" he said.

"Right, Sheriff, you'll see, and—"

"And I suppose, while you were listening in on that conversation, you found out why they kidnapped Gunther Waldorf?"

"It's something to do with a survey he made of the Shinnecock reservation land, Sheriff. Some secret study the Citizens' Committee wants because they need it to get at the oil reserves and so on offshore and inland."

The Sheriff rubbed his lean face. "Oh, boy," he said.

"And so if they don't get Waldorf to talk, they're gonna create their own incident, somebody said, like starting a fire to get in there and take over the oil and mineral deposits. I think Calloway was in charge of that for the corporation—"

"For the who?"

"The corporation. I guess they're the ones behind

all this—" From the den, I heard the announcer on TV yelling something, a bell ringing, a lot of cheering. "I think your fight is over in there."

"Figures," he said. He pulled on his squall coat Strapped on his gun. "Come on. Get in the car."

It was my turn to stare. "You mean you believe me?"

"Get in the car," he ordered.

I held out the recorder again. "Don't you want to hear it first?"

He shook his head. "We can hear it later. If you've got it all down, that's fine and dandy. Did Yerkos ever find out what you were about? Peeking out through that trapdoor, you said."

"Well, we got a break there, Sheriff. I don't think so. Everything was going great with his trance up to the point the ghost came."

Sheriff Landry closed his eyes. "The ghost?"

"Yeah, my pirate ghost, Redbeard. Captain Marion, the one who wants me to find him his gold. Mrs. Teska's sister Sofi—the one who died—well, her spirit was there telling Mrs. Teska to give everything she had to Yerkos, because she would be dying soon. I think she wrote out a check to Yerkos, but when she signed the paper, the ghost came, and he got mad. Telling her she didn't have the right to give away what was really his, and—"

"She signed the paper?"

I found it in my pocket and unfolded it. He grabbed it out of my hand. "Nothing signed here," he said. "She just got a word or two down— 'I, Anna Teska, am giving—' "

"Well, that's when the ghost came and took it out

of her hands. And then he chased her sister Sofi's spirit
—and then he came across the room toward me with
the paper—and that's when Solo Yerkos got up, but I
don't know if he ever saw me."

The Sheriff opened the door. An icy blast blew into
the house. "Get in the car," he repeated. "I know I'll
regret this later. But right now, if I hear any more,
I'm ready for the loony bin."

I started after him. "You'll see, Sheriff, I was right
after all."

"This time you better be," he said.

The moon came out from behind some thin clouds.
The sky was full of twinkling stars. It was cold in the
Sheriff's car, and the grim look on his taut face didn't
make the ride any more comfortable. He had his big
foot down to the floor of his souped-up old Pontiac,
and the big engine roared as we tore down the back
streets.

He never said another word, didn't ask me any more
questions, and the mean look on his face kept me from
talking. The Old King Dick house was only ten
minutes away from the Sheriff's in King's Point, but he
made it in less. At the final turn on Hellsfire, he had
the car cornering on two wheels, but I didn't say anything about that, either.

The house was still lit. The Sheriff's car roared up
and scattered dust as the wheels locked to a skidding
stop. He got out his side of the car, taking long strides
to the door without waiting for me, and I hurried out
after him. He banged on the door with his fist, not

bothering with the bronze knocker, and almost instantly I could hear footsteps coming across the room inside.

The door opened and Solo Yerkos stood there. He looked at me without expression and then at the Sheriff. "Yes?" he said.

"I'm Sheriff Landry. Hampton police. Report of a disturbance."

The door swung wider without delay. "Come in," Yerkos said. He extended one hand toward the inner rooms, and as we passed, shut the door behind us.

The entry hall was dimly lit. A tall wood clothestree was covered with heavy clothing. We followed Solo Yerkos into the dining room. A gray-haired man sat at the long rosewood table, his back to us.

"There must be some mistake, officer," Solo Yerkos said. "I'm here alone with just an old friend visiting me. Perhaps you already know each other. If not—Sheriff Landry, this is Gunther Waldorf."

The man turned to face us and smiled. I nearly fell right through the floor. He didn't look drugged. He didn't look hypnotized, or feverish, or sick. He didn't look much like a prisoner, either.

He sat up straight as if filled with vitality, clear-eyed, with a healthy, ruddy complexion. His hands rested calmly on the arms of the tufted red Jacobean chair.

I wanted to send a silent message to the Sheriff. Like, don't look, it's a trick. This is the wrong Gunther Waldorf. The real one is downstairs nearly dying in the prayer room.

But apparently Sheriff Landry didn't read my thoughts. He nodded coolly to the gray-haired man and turned to Yerkos. "Sorry," he said. "Guess we got the wrong address."

No, no, I wanted to say. It's the right address. But the wrong Gunther Waldorf.

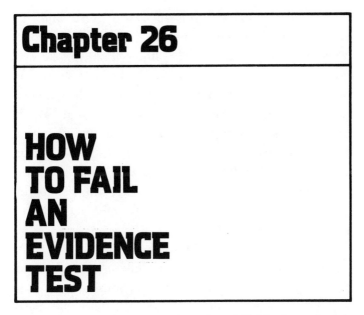

Chapter 26

HOW TO FAIL AN EVIDENCE TEST

The man introduced as Gunther Waldorf made his eyes seem to twinkle from behind his steel-rimmed glasses. "For a moment, Sheriff, I thought you were collecting autographs again." He looked at me and lost the twinkle. "Ah, it is you again! We are seeing much of each other lately."

I felt the Sheriff's eyes boring into me. "I asked him to autograph another of his books for me the other night," I explained. "Now Minerva and I each have Gunther Waldorf's signature."

The gray-haired man laughed. "Ah, yes, Minerva—I remember that name." Rumpling my hair playfully but with a heavy hand, he smiled at the Sheriff. "Does this boy always travel with you? He wants to be a policeman too, some day, perhaps?"

Sheriff Landry nodded with a thin smile and spoke

curtly. "I'm breaking him in early. Steve and my daughter are old friends. Grew up together." He ignored Yerkos and his friend and his hot yellow wolflike eyes quartered the downstairs rooms. At the far end, in darkness, was the old sitting room parlor. The trapdoor was under a Hepplewhite table, I saw now, and covered by a small scatter rug. The curtain on the right that had illuminated the dancing spirit of Mrs. Teska's sister was gone. I saw a hall and a staircase.

Sheriff Landry frowned. "Obviously there's no disturbance here. Wonder if I got the right address? On Hellsfire, number 1111 . . ."

Solo Yerkos waved his hands. "I think I can explain. We did have a seance a while ago—perhaps an hour or so. And as sometimes is the case, emotions run high. The spirits who visit us talk, and the party anxious to make contact with the other world sometimes is overcome. I, myself, am in a trance state then, not actually aware of what is going on. In this world, yes, but also in part of the other."

I saw a chance to get into the conversation. "I guess that must have been Mrs. Teska, Sheriff. She told me she had an appointment here about eight o'clock this evening. Something about hoping to contact her dead sister's spirit."

"Could that have been it, Mr. Yerkos?" Sheriff Landry asked.

Yerkos bowed slightly. "It must have been. It was the only seance we had tonight. And if you know Mrs. Teska, you must also know she is an extremely old woman—"

"Yes, and an amazingly healthy one. Very spry for her age," Sheriff Landry said. "I only hope I'm that good myself if I ever pass my seventies."

Yerkos's eyes glittered. "Yes, for her age she is quite good. That is, physically. However, this evening was a very trying emotional experience for her. In fact, she broke down afterward and had to be helped out."

"Mrs. Teska doesn't own a car," the Sheriff said. "I hope you saw to it that she got home all right."

"Yes. Of course. I called a taxi to drive her home."

"Good," the Sheriff said. He put his hand on my shoulder. "Steve is very close to Mrs. Teska. Known her since he could walk. Naturally, he was concerned about her well-being, too."

Yerkos nodded. "Quite understandable. And commendable, too, a boy his age with concern for an elderly woman."

"I think so, too," the Sheriff said. "And her sister's spirit actually made an appearance tonight?"

Yerkos folded his hands, and bowed his head reverently. "Tonight was most successful. The spirit was here, obeying my invocation for its appearance. I can remember that, but later, I lost consciousness. When I awoke, the spirit had gone. Mrs. Teska was weeping uncontrollably."

Sheriff Landry turned to the gray-haired man. "Were you present during the seance, Professor Waldorf?"

"No, I only just arrived. I wanted to consult with my friend Solo about another matter."

"That's interesting," the Sheriff said. "A famous ecologist with a brilliant scientific background together with a medium and psychic, who can flaunt your laws and make the unexplainable happen."

The gray-haired man shrugged, smiling. "The more one learns about this world, the more uncertain one is about what he knows."

Sheriff Landry showed his long wolfish teeth in a smile. "Ain't it the truth!" He looked at his wristwatch. "Sorry to have taken so much of your time, gentlemen. I can give you a lift back home, Mr. Waldorf, if you would be leaving fairly soon. We can wait outside."

The so-called Waldorf waved his hand. "No, thanks, officer. I have my own car."

Sheriff Landry looked surprised. "I didn't see one parked outside."

"It's parked way back in the driveway," the man said.

"Well, in that case, we'll be leaving. Sorry again to disturb you." As Yerkos moved, the Sheriff said, "Don't bother. I can find my own way out."

Yerkos bowed stiffly, and the man who looked like Waldorf waved his hand. We passed into the entry hall, and as we went by the clothes rack there, Sheriff Landry surprised me by poking my ribs with his elbow.

His voice was low and mocking, close to my ear, when he said, "If you notice, he did better this time." I looked up at him puzzled and his low voice continued. "He remembered to wear his overcoat."

I rolled my eyes to the rack. He wasn't kidding.

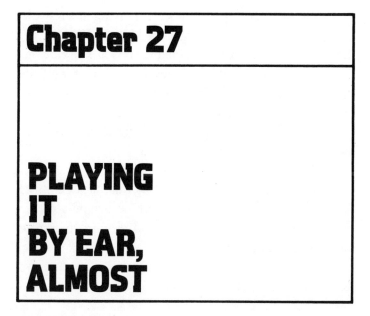

Chapter 27

PLAYING IT BY EAR, ALMOST

The Sheriff sat stiffly in the car, his big hands hooked over the wheel. He stared out through the windshield toward the dimly lit houses farther down on Hellsfire Street. I waited for him to start the car, get me back to his house, then throw me out for wasting his time. Instead, he just sat.

Finally he leaned back, his long fingers drumming on the wheel. "I know what you're thinking I'm thinking," he said in his harsh growling voice, "but you're wrong."

"You do?" I said. "I mean, I am?"

"You bet. You're thinking that I'm down on you again. That you goofed again. That you let your imagination run away with you. Right?"

"Well, yeah. I wouldn't blame you. There he was looking the picture of health after my telling you he was drugged and sick, and held prisoner down there."

He nodded, still staring ahead, making no move to get away from the Old King Dick house. "It's too pat," he said. "Too much of a coincidence. I'm still not buying what you said, but what they showed me didn't ring right with me. Something phony there. Trouble is, I just can't put my finger on it."

"Maybe this will help," I said. "That guy who says he's Gunther Waldorf made one big mistake there."

"If he did, I never noticed it."

"He said he had his car parked out back. Gunther Waldorf didn't drive. I don't think he owned a car."

Sheriff Landry whipped his head around to stare at me. "You sure about that?"

I shrugged. "Pretty sure. I never saw him in one. But more important, it was against what he believed in to own or drive a car."

"What's that?"

"Pollution, Sheriff. You know how strong he was on anything fouling up the air we breathe. Minerva has read more of his books than I have. She can tell you how he was always raving against our using up our precious natural resources to foul the environment."

"That a fact?" he muttered. He reached out and picked up a microphone. Flipping the switch, he said, "Landry here. I'd like a quick check run with the DMV. Gunther Waldorf. Tupelo Lane. Hampton resident past ten years. I want make of vehicle, time of purchase, license number, and date of registration. Get back to me fast, sergeant."

The filtered voice came in on the radio saying, "Will do," and Sheriff Landry hung up the mike. "It will take a while," he said. He held his hand out toward me. I started to shake it before he checked me. "Let's see what you've got on your recorder. Got both sessions, you said. The committee and Mrs. Teska's seance, right?"

"Right, Sheriff, up to the part where the ghost came in and I panicked."

He took the recorder in his big hands and pressed the "play" button. There was a light whirring sound. "Hold it," I said, "I forgot to rewind. I didn't have time, Sheriff."

He handed it back and I pressed the "rewind" button until the tape stopped whirring. "Okay, now it ought to be ready," I said, pressing the "play" button.

The Sheriff held it as the tape whirred and hummed. There was a low murmur. "That's the big guy. Joe, I think. He's telling Calloway they're set to go against the Indians."

The low murmuring voice stopped. Not a word could be understood. Sheriff Landry looked at me. Another murmur sounded.

"That's Brad Case, Sheriff. He was worried they were going too fast. And he wanted Mr. Calloway's opinion."

Again, the recorder picked up nothing but distant sounds. There was a soft clink. "I think I hit the recorder then on the trapdoor hinge, trying to get closer. You'll hear Calloway now telling how they can't hold Waldorf prisoner forever. How Simpson at the house was getting nervous."

Sheriff Landry nodded and listened. Calloway's voice was a distant mumble. A series of sounds too far off to hear. I felt foolish. There was another noise and tapping. "That's Yerkos, I think. Telling how Waldorf won't talk about the private study he made of the Shinnecock oil and mineral deposits."

Sheriff Landry shook his head and began moving the dial on the side of the recorder to its loudest pitch. It brought out the murmuring sounds a little clearer, but no distinct words or sentences. Then there was a drumming and slapping sound.

"That's the big guy, Joe, again. He's saying that the Indians won't let any more studies be made of their land, and that they'll just have to go in there by provoking an incident."

Sheriff Landry looked at me. I shrugged, wishing I could disappear. The tape kept spinning, humming. There wasn't any question about some conversation being held someplace. But what anybody said remained a mystery.

I was about to explain again when the Sheriff held up his hand to stop me. A voice came through. "—answer your question, Brad?" Then it became inaudible again.

"That was Calloway," I said. "He's saying they had too much at stake to wait any longer and had to make their own opening now."

Sheriff Landry had the receiver close against his face, half in his ear, and nodded sourly. The tape hummed and whirred and the sounds came and went. I could still see it all in my mind but that wasn't helping my case any with the Sheriff. The tape spun on, humming.

"Somewhere around here Brad Case got worried

about what Calloway was going to do. Calloway said they'd start a fire or two. It would stir up the people, make them think the Indians were wasting their precious oil."

Sheriff Landry nodded patiently. I could tell the whole thing was a total bust, a disaster, but he stuck with it. At intervals now, he stopped the tape to let me explain.

"There was this guy they got at the Bureau of Indian Affairs," I said. "He was supposed to help them get away with it."

He punched the button and the tape hummed some more. He hit the "stop" button and looked across the seat at me.

"I think that was the place where Yerkos still thought he could get Waldorf to talk about what he knows. And then Calloway got mad and said he had only till the middle of next week. They had to go ahead with the corporation plan to drill."

Landry looked at me. The tape hummed and spun some more.

"Now they're worried about Simpson giving himself away to some nosy reporter."

Landry listened again and then stopped it, shaking his head.

"Now they're talking about Mrs. Teska. Yerkos is saying she's due soon. How he doesn't expect trouble getting her to sign over her holdings, the property they're interested in."

"Yerkos said that?"

"Yeah, and the big guy got nasty and said she was

an old lady, and ought to be a cinch for him. They're mad at him for not getting Gunther Waldorf to talk."

The Sheriff nodded, his face relaxed now, and I felt a bit easier about goofing this way. He let the tape run and run. "I guess this is the part with Mrs. Teska," he said. We both strained our ears trying to pick up something.

There was a light tinkling sound. A soft laugh. "That's her spirit, Sofi. Her dead sister talking now. Telling her to give everything away to Solo Yerkos."

Sheriff Landry nodded glumly. He let the tape run. There were just indistinct sounds, murmurs, and silences. "Too far away," he said once. "Tough luck, Steve."

At one point there was a loud noise, followed by a faint scream. Sheriff Landry cocked his head at me. "Your ghost?"

I nodded. "Yeah, he scared off her sister Sofi's spirit then, and then he grabbed the paper away from Mrs. Teska—" There was a loud noise.

"What is this—who are you?"

I clapped my hands. "That's Yerkos. Listen."

The tape spun and only hummed again. I gritted my teeth. "Well, that's where the ghost is telling him they can't give away something that belonged to him. About his gold that's in there."

Sheriff Landry didn't say anything more. He let the tape spin to the end. Nothing more came out. All that good stuff I thought I had down there, proof of what these crooks were doing.

The Sheriff handed the recorder back. "Too bad you

didn't let Herky rig up a listening bug for you. He could have given you something to plant there that could pick up the voices a quarter of a mile away."

I shook my head dolefully. "Yeah, I know. I thought I could do it myself. It was real stupid on my part, I know."

"Tough luck," he said. "You might have had something that could have stood up in court. We could have nailed them, and you would have been a real hero."

"Well, you still got the real Gunther Waldorf down there," I said. "Locked up in the prayer room, the basement. Why don't you just go back in and find him? You're the law."

"That's how they do it on TV or the movies," he said harshly. "No way I can go back in there without a search warrant. Anyway, you still haven't proved a thing to me about anything. It's all hearsay. Not a shred of real evidence."

"What about that car thing? Won't that do it, if they check back with you and say Gunther Waldorf never owned a car."

Sheriff Landry nodded. "That would be something to go on. I'll give them a few more minutes to see what they can dig up."

"And if he's got a car registered to his name?"

The Sheriff spread his hands apart. "Then you've got nothing."

I thought I heard something. "Would you mind opening your window, Sheriff?"

He looked sharply at me. "Are you crazy? It's cold outside."

"I know. I thought I heard something—from the house."

He shrugged and turned his window down. He cocked his head, frowning in concentration. "Like what?"

The sound came again. "There! Don't you hear that?"

He put his head out the window. "You're too wound up about all this. That's just the sound of a barking dog."

I nodded. "Yeah. Only this one is mine—it's Sinbad."

He stared at me, listening carefully again. The sound came once more, deep and rumbling. "Are you sure? How could he get in there?"

I shook my head. "He's not exactly in there. From the sound, he's *down* there. *Down in the prayer room.*"

He frowned. "How could he get down there?"

"I don't know, Sheriff," I said. "Unless Minerva brought him with her."

Then I was out of his car and running for the back of the old Garrison Colonial. I heard the Sheriff calling for me to stop, to come back. But this time I didn't listen.

Sinbad only barks that way when he's in trouble.

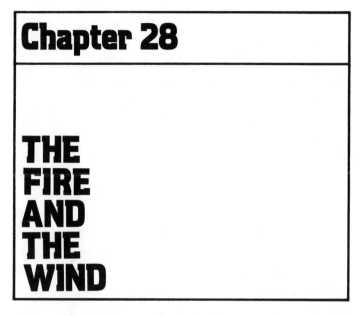

Chapter 28

THE FIRE AND THE WIND

The wintry night wind was sweeping across Jonah's Bay in fierce gusts. As I came toward the rear of the house perched high on the exposed bluff, the force nearly blew me down. The Sheriff was behind me yelling something, but his words were lost in the whistling sound of the wind.

The fake well was where I had left it, off center. But the lid to the underground passage was pushed aside. As I climbed down the iron rungs of the short ladder, I wondered if I was being baited into a trap. The notion of Sinbad down there didn't make sense. Then I heard his deep booming bark again, and sense or not, I knew he was there. I still couldn't be certain about Minerva being along.

As my head was dipping below ground level, I saw

Sheriff Landry running toward me. His long legs were flying, the wide beam of his flashlight bouncing over the ground. Waving his arms, he yelled again. But I figured this was my own deal now, not his or the law's, and stepped down the rest of the rungs.

The tunnel was as cold, dark, and damp as it had been before. But where it ended at the chimney foundation, something was different. The heavy timber shoring at the sides had somehow loosened. A big 12x12 roofing beam had slipped and fallen across the passageway.

It had partly closed the narrow space to the door of the prayer room and was wedged squarely against it. The area I had crawled through to find the entrance was now partially covered by the clay and moist earth the beam had dislodged when it fell. What it amounted to was that if Minerva was in there with Sinbad, she couldn't get out now with all that weight against the door.

Sinbad's booming bark sounded again, and I was afraid to answer him, not knowing who might be down there with them. The beam was too heavy for me to move, and I dropped to my knees and clawed away at the pile of dirt, shoveling it aside, trying to clear a path.

The blinding light of the Sheriff's police flashlight hit me in the eyes then, and he came up behind it. He was breathing hard, and his voice sounded tense and angry. "This better not be another of your wild ideas," he growled, and then Sinbad barked again. The Sheriff stiffened and listened, cocking his head. Then he sighed. "Guess you're right, Steve. I know that bark. What's the problem here?"

I pointed out the door entrance and the heavy beam blocking it. "If they're inside, the only way they can get out is up through the trapdoor," I whispered. "And we don't know if Solo Yerkos knows about this exit door or not, yet. Maybe he thinks the prayer room there where he's got Waldorf is just a basement for the house. Minerva must have tried to get back out when the beam fell, found out she was trapped, and that's why Sinbad is barking."

"Could be," he rasped. "She knew we were heading here. But she'll have to come up with a mighty good excuse for being here."

I scooped some dirt up and threw it to the side. "Maybe she found more evidence in his garbage can."

He was thrusting against the big beam with all his strength. He stopped and glared angrily at me. "What?"

"Minerva went through Gunther Waldorf's garbage cans there at his house. She found out the new Waldorf is a meat-eater, not a vegetarian like the real Waldorf inside there."

He tugged at the beam again. "You kids are going crazy."

"It checks," I said. "Like the phony Waldorf upstairs using a car."

He stepped aside, checking the angle of the beam against the door, then gave me his flashlight. "We'll see about that," he said. "Now here's what I want you to do. Hold the light up here so I can gauge how much I need to push it aside to get us in there."

I put the flash up and he rubbed his big hands together. "Okay, this is too heavy for me to handle alone.

You push now with me and lift. When there's enough clearance you get the door open and slip inside."

I shook my head. "You can't hold that beam alone, Sheriff. It'll crush you."

His teeth grated and his voice was hot and harsh. "Do as I say. I'll try to flip it aside long enough for me to get through behind you."

When Sheriff Landry gives you an order in that mean tone of voice, you don't argue. "Okay," I said. I took the big flashlight and tucked it under my belt. That was when I discovered I had taken along the medicine bag Dark Cloud had given me, and somehow it made me feel stronger.

The beam lay at an upright angle solidly against the door at an angle of about forty-five degrees. We had to lift it straight up for me to get the door open. Then the Sheriff had to balance it somehow until he could get inside behind me. I couldn't believe he or any man would be able to hold that weight by himself.

But then Minerva screamed from inside the room and Sinbad barked furiously, the rolling awesome sound of thunder rolling in his big chest.

Sheriff Landry said just one word. "Go!"

I put all my weight and strength into it, and he got under with his shoulder. Slowly the beam went up and up, and our breathing got awfully loud as we strained against the weight. Then it was cleared enough for me to reach out for the door. I pulled it forward. "Okay," I said. "I'm cutting out."

There was no way I could help him now, and I jumped inside the room. He held the beam for a moment, arms locked under it, his breath rasping and heavy. Then he took a quick deep breath, and with a sudden movement, he pushed it up higher and slightly to the side. In that split second he dived for the opening. I saw the tight triumphant grin on his face as he came through, and then the door slammed shut as the beam fell back against it, sealing us all in.

Minerva came running over, Sinbad at her side. She leaned down. "Pop, are you okay?"

He looked up, still breathing heavily, the wind knocked out of him, and nodded. He sat up slowly, shaking his head. "What was all that screaming about?"

She half-turned, pointing over her shoulder. I put the flashlight beam there. Gunther Waldorf was sitting up, looking ghastly in the light, moaning, blinking his eyes behind those steel-rimmed glasses. "I thought he was a ghost!"

Sheriff Landry got up, took the flash from me, and walked toward the narrow cot. Waldorf fell back weakly before he was near. Sheriff Landry looked closely into his eyes, and then leaned down to take his pulse.

"Well, do you believe now that he was kidnapped?" Minerva said.

Sheriff Landry shook his head, growling. "One thing at a time, Minerva. We'll iron out the details later." He walked back to the door and tried opening it, without any luck. He glanced sourly at me. "That was a pretty dumb move on my part," he said. "I thought I had it set to drop aside, clearing the door." Minerva had her flashlight along, too, and with all the beams on, we were able to see the whole prayer room. His eyes shifted toward the ladder and the trapdoor above. "Cool it," he said softly. "Company's coming."

The trapdoor was opening, the lid was drawn back, and the thin dark-clad figure of Solo Yerkos came down through the aperture.

Sinbad stepped quickly in front of me and Minerva. A deep menacing growl came rumbling from his chest. Yerkos had already taken his next step down on the ladder, and now he froze. He was holding a kerosene lantern, and he lifted it outward. The light illuminated most of the prayer room. He saw Sinbad, and then his eyes shifted to the end of the room where I stood with Minerva and Sheriff Landry.

Yerkos looked shocked, his face contorted behind the glow of his lantern. "What's the meaning of this?" he shouted. "How did you people get in here?" Then his eyes fastened on me. The secret of the passageway I carried in my head wasn't any secret to him, apparently. He read my mind in a split second, as if I had big signs hanging out telling him all he wanted to know. He nodded. "Of course! There is a secret underground passageway."

Sheriff Landry lifted his torch and held the beam on Yerkos. "I'm afraid there's a little explaining you'll have to do, Mr. Yerkos." His beam swung across the room to the cot holding Gunther Waldorf. "You can start with the man on the bed there who bears a remarkable resemblance to the man you introduced me to earlier as Gunther Waldorf."

Minerva couldn't keep still another moment. "I'm

telling you this is the real Gunther Waldorf, Pop. Steve and I know it. You're the only one who's not with it."

The medium stiffened. He raised his lantern higher as if to get a better look at Minerva.

But Sinbad had a different idea. He must have thought that Yerkos was threatening Minerva. He growled his deep-throated challenge, legs bowed out, his hooked lower fangs outthrust. Then with flattened ears, head lowered, he thundered across the room toward Yerkos high on the ladder.

No ladder was ever built that could withstand the terrible force of Sinbad's charge. This one was a couple of hundred years old, and the wood dried out. As Sinbad leaped up, hitting it, the old wood splintered, cracked, and then suddenly came apart.

Solo Yerkos screamed as the pole ends separated. He grabbed for the top ends, as the rungs under his feet gave way. The kerosene lamp dropped out of his hands, hit the floor, and then exploded like a bombshell in a blinding burst of flame.

Yerkos screamed again, dangling helplessly in the air above the quick blaze, and then grabbed desperately for the open trapdoor. His body swayed, and swung erratically, as the ladder fell away from him and crashed to the floor. Yerkos's grip held. Then he pulled himself up and disappeared through the opening in the ceiling.

I heard the Sheriff yelling and realized suddenly I was so fascinated watching Yerkos avoid falling down, I forgot that the prayer room was now on fire.

Sheriff Landry's long arm swept out, knocking Minerva and me aside. "Get away," he yelled. He ran for the bed, yanked the blanket off Waldorf, and rushed back toward the flames. As he beat at the flames, he yelled at me, "Work on the door. We're trapped!"

The flames danced higher and licked at the ceiling, the updraft sucking them higher. "Yerkos," the Sheriff yelled, "throw down a rope or some sheets."

There was the sound of running feet above the flames and the trapdoor slammed shut. I was at the tunnel door putting all my weight against it, calling Sinbad back from the flames. When the trapdoor dropped, closing us in, I realized suddenly that everything happening now, everybody's life being in danger, was all my fault.

Minerva rushed over to my side, trying to help me budge the door. "It's stuck," I told her. "There's a big beam that fell on the other side. It's wedged against the door, Minerva. No way this can open."

Sinbad was barking furiously against the advancing flames, stepping back as they came at him, charging forward at other menacing flames. "Sinbad, come back here," I yelled, but he was too excited to listen.

The Sheriff was swinging the blanket like a wild man trying to stamp out and smother the flames. The entire room was of wood, old and so dry it burned like paper. As I watched the sheriff put out a small section of the fire, it came back to life as if by magic. It began to spread, an army of leaping little flames.

Minerva yelled, "I better get back to Mr. Waldorf and keep the fire off him."

He was sitting, shaking, helpless to do anything against the advancing flames. I pounded the door with my shoulder but it was jammed solid. The wall lining the tunnel was of joined planks, and I went down the line kicking and pounding at them, hoping to splinter one and break through. But the pine wall was solid. I was getting nowhere. The fire was spreading around the room, despite the efforts of the Sheriff and Minerva.

The end poles of the ladder were charred, and burning, too. There was no way to open the trapdoor overhead, and the smoke burned my eyes. Minerva was coughing from it as she swatted the flames with rags from the corner of the room. I was getting dizzy from the heat.

Sinbad was slowing down, losing some of his pep and strength. He charged each new dancing flame, barking furiously at it, and then backing off as it licked at him. I had a terrible feeling that we were all going to end up as charred and burned as the wooden ladder.

Suddenly my mind switched to Dark Cloud and his last words to me. "The Great Spirit has spoken, my son. The test is yet to come. Your own spirit will tell you how to stand in the path of the fire that devours all."

I had to admit Dark Cloud hadn't lost his gift of prophecy, because what we had here was certainly that kind of fire.

But Dark Cloud had said my spirit would find a way to deal with it. Maybe he overestimated me. All I had done so far was collect a bunch of bruises pounding my body at the walls. I had to keep testing each part though, because sometimes in their old houses, the early colonists constructed sliding panels controlled by balance beams. If you found the right spot, you could trigger the mechanism. The escape route would be behind it.

Whoever had built this prayer room had done a good job with the tunnel out to the rear of the house. I was hoping he wasn't satisfied with that one, that he was the worrying type, and that he decided to carve another way out, just in case, that would lead to the beach and water below the bluff.

The flames were dotting the room, dancing closer. Minerva and the Sheriff kept slapping away at them with their blanket and rags. It was getting awfully hot, harder to breathe.

I came to the short end wall closest to the bay, trying my luck every inch of the way, pushing and prodding each plank. I saw Gunther Waldorf shaking as if he had the flu bug. He was on a straw mattress, I suddenly realized, an easy treat for the flames. I reached out and yanked him and the cot toward me, where the fire still hadn't attacked. A burning wisp of paper flew across the room over my head. It landed on the short wall near the cot. I rushed over to brush it off. As I did, my hand felt a cool current of air coming from a narrow chink between the vertical pine wallboards.

Excited, I bent closer. I heard it then, a high whistling sound, felt it cooling my face.

The wind!

The automatic replay set in my head switched on again. Dark Cloud was pressing something soft into my hand. His deep sonorous voice sounded in my ears again, as if I was still there with him on the Shinnecock reservation. "Your heart will listen to the whispering wind of the Great Spirit. Use this, my son, when you hear the wind speaking to you."

The heat of the prayer room was intense now, almost unbearable. I could hear Minerva shouting, her father answering, as if from a great distance. But I was standing there like a dummy, not doing anything to help, simply staring down at the old deerskin medicine bag Dark Cloud had given me.

Wondering how to use my Indian magic.

Chapter 29

HOW TO DO INDIAN MAGIC

I was sitting on the floor when Sinbad trotted over. Smoke was coming from his feet. I lifted them carefully to make sure none of his hair was on fire. His feet felt hot and the pads looked scorched and blackened with soot. "I warned you," I told him, "but you wouldn't listen. You can't be such a wise guy running around in fire when you don't wear shoes."

I spit on my fingers and rubbed them on his feet, wetting them down some, cooling them off. He didn't whimper but I could tell he felt guilty about being so dumb. I showed him the deerskin pouch. "Here's that sacred old medicine bag the Indian chief Dark Cloud gave me, remember? He told me to use it and it would work. Only he didn't tell me how."

Sinbad sniffed and came closer as I poured the contents of the pouch out into my other hand. I didn't know how to make any speech or prayer to the Great Spirit as Dark Cloud did. And I didn't want to fake one, either. So I just sat there looking at the little colored and bleached stones, the small dried bones, the shreds of colored feathers, some glass beads.

"We got to say some kind of prayer to get us out of here," I told Sinbad, "or else we get fried to a crisp. Maybe you can think of something."

He poked his dark muzzle excitedly into my hand. The feather must have tickled his nose and he sneezed. A small red bead fell to the floor. "Now look what you did," I told him. "We need all this stuff for the Great Spirit."

Sinbad slapped at the rolling bead with his big paw but it bounced away. He went after it but it rolled to the wall and fell into a crack. Sinbad sniffed and whimpered. His big feet began scraping the plank where the bead had fallen through. "Forget it," I told him. "We don't have time. Now we'll have to do it without that one."

But Sinbad never gives up. He kept working at the plank with his big feet, and in his excitement his hard head hit the wall. There was a loud clicking sound, a rumble, and the wall moved.

"You did it!" I yelled. I turned toward the Sheriff. "Come on," I shouted, "Sinbad found it." I jumped up tugging at the wall. The opening was too narrow to get through, and it locked where it was.

Sheriff Landry turned to look at me. His face was haggard, sweaty, blackened with soot. He didn't seem to understand what I was saying, and he turned back impatiently to fight the fire.

I called to Minerva. "Sinbad found the secret opening. Come over, quick!"

Minerva's eyes widened as she saw the dark opening in the wall. She dropped her smoking rags, and came running across the room. She had to run around the cot with Gunther Waldorf on it, and she tripped on some of the old junk in the corner. To keep from falling, she threw her arms out, clutching at the planked wall.

There was another loud click, a rumbling noise, and she screamed happily, "It's opening! Pop, look! We found it!"

He turned his head, annoyed, but then he must have felt the wind. It swept across the room driving the flames higher. He crouched under the glare of the flame, rubbed his eyes, and stared hard for a moment. He took a few steps forward, and then he recovered and became chief of police again, barking out orders.

"Okay, Minerva. Get out first with Sinbad and hold on to your flashlight. Steve, give me a hand here with Waldorf."

It was the first time he had admitted it!

Sinbad charged through the opening, barking, excited at the new scent. It was damp and salty, something you couldn't mistake—the smell of the bay water.

Minerva followed Sinbad, playing her flashlight on the tunnel walls. I was behind her holding up Gunther Waldorf's ankles while Sheriff Landry carried the rest of him. The passage was dark and narrow with barely enough space to squeeze through. It opened gradually into a natural high-vaulted cave.

Minerva's form was silhouetted ahead of me. Suddenly she disappeared. I nearly dropped Waldorf.

"Minerva," I yelled. "What happened?"

The Sheriff pushed forward and we began to run. Her voice came echoing back off the walls. "Look out for the big drop there."

The warning came too late and I fell down, dragging Waldorf and Sheriff Landry after me. The floor of the cave dropped so sharply under our feet, it was as if we had fallen into a deep hole or cavern. Minerva yelled again. "It's all downhill now."

The soft clay under our feet was slippery, and we stumbled over rocks and clumps of earth fallen from the cavern walls. It was tough going. But soon the burning heat and fear of the prayer room had receded to a point far behind us, and the gusty chill wind howling through the long winding cave felt good.

I had an idea where we would be coming out. Somewhere along the beach near the Jonah Jaws cave of old Captain Billy Murdock. I had walked along the beachfront with Sinbad many times, investigating everything that looked as if it could be another cave, but never with any luck.

The Jonah Jaws cave could be approached only by water through a five-pointed rock opening according to the tides. If you didn't know the tides, you could drown in there. What would happen here, I thought, if, when we came to the end, the cave opening was blocked?

Minerva's piercing wail from somewhere ahead told me I was worrying on the right track. "It's closed up—there's no way out!"

We came up and laid Gunther Waldorf down short of the dead end. Sheriff Landry looked him over. "The poor guy's taken a beating bouncing along on this trip, plus what he's had before. The sooner we get him to a hospital, the better."

I moved up to a giant rock surrounded by big boulders, sealing the entrance. "Yeah, only we got to move this first." Behind the large stones I could imagine tons of earth eroded from the cliff wall above. Only small crevices between the rock formation allowed the wind to whip through.

Sheriff Landry spit on his big hands, rubbed them together, and braced against the rock. He pushed with all his strength, and I joined him, using everything I had, but the rock didn't budge. We tried again, this time with Minerva adding her muscle and weight, and Sinbad was barking and trying to dig a trench under it, but none of the rocks would budge for all our combined tugging.

Sheriff Landry called a halt. "Let's take a break. We have plenty of air, and maybe after a rest, we'll be able to figure a way out."

Minerva joined him as he checked Gunther Waldorf's pulse and eyes. Then Sheriff Landry asked me if I remembered what Solo Yerkos had been doing to him to make him talk. "Mind-control drugs, plus some hypnotism, Sheriff."

He sat down, head back against the cave wall, looking

beat. "Well, that's reversible," he said. "POWs had it, and they came out of it okay."

I took out the deerskin pouch again, and sat down near the rocks. Sinbad caught the scent of it immediately and came over, sniffing excitedly.

"Just watch it now," I told him. "You got lucky back there in the prayer room and found the way out. But you also cost me one of Dark Cloud's red beads. So it's okay to look but don't touch."

Minerva came over to sit beside me. "What's that you've got there?"

I showed it to her. "Dark Cloud, the old Shinnecock medicine man, gave it to me. It's his sacred spirits bag."

Her eyes rolled. "Oh, brother!" she said.

"Don't kid about it," I said. "It got us out of that fire in the prayer room, didn't it?"

"Are you for real?" she hooted. "I did it when I fell against the wall and hit something with my hand. That was me, not that dopey bag of horsefeathers."

"Well, yeah, you helped," I admitted. "But how do we know Dark Cloud's sacred spirits didn't make you trip and fall on the wall, and hit it at just the right place?"

"Oh, brother," she said again. "You know, you're turning into a real nut lately."

I waved the pouchskin. "Okay, just watch and see, Minerva. I'm going to ask Dark Cloud for his help again. You just sit there where you are. Don't do anything. I don't want you taking credit for my Indian magic."

She moved back against the wall. "Is this far enough or do you want me to go back up the hill?"

"That's fine, Minerva," I said. "Now don't interrupt. I got to concentrate on this."

She touched her lips with her fingers, grinning.

"Okay," I said. "Remember you promised not to move or say anything. I don't want those spirits thinking I don't believe this stuff."

"What's happening there?" her pop asked her.

"He's got a medicine bag," she said. "He's going to call down some spirits to get us out of here."

"Well," Sheriff Landry said, "don't knock it. It sounds like a good idea."

"Are you kidding? What kind of Indian is he?" she said.

He waved his hands, and leaned back against the wall, exhausted. "So far, he hasn't done that badly," he murmured, and closed his eyes.

I dumped all the stuff out of the bag. Sinbad slid down to his favorite flying-squirrel position, his dark muzzle outstretched toward the little pile of bones, beads, and feathers but not touching anything. He waited quietly, as he did whenever we conducted a meeting.

"Okay," I said, "here goes. Don't sneeze or anything. I think what we have to do now is some kind of meditation. Dogs can probably do it, too. Just wish we all were outside these rocks and running free down along the beach and the water. Okay? Here goes."

Sinbad's eyes glowed with that mysterious love light in the darkness. His stubby tail thumped, telling me he trusted as well as loved me. Well, I had to come through for him, too. Especially since he was so brave back there, fighting the fire and getting his dumb feet burned.

I closed my eyes. I concentrated on the image of Dark Cloud, visualizing him exactly as I had seen him last with his craggy, leathery, wrinkled face, the iron-gray steady eyes, the long hair tumbling to his broad shoulders. I had to find some way of letting him know what was happening, and maybe some of his friendly spirits would be tuning in and give us a helping hand.

"Well, Dark Cloud," I said to myself, "remember me, the friend of George Cooper, who is the son of Angry Runner, who was the son of Straight Path, and so on? We got away from that man you showed me in your magic fire, that Nameless One, and I heard the wind like you said, after the fire came to devour us. I used my heart, like your Great Spirit said, and your spirit bag, and we got out of there okay.

"But now we're stuck just at the end of this cave by some rocks that weigh a ton, and we can't move them to get out. The wind is whispering to me again, kind of whistling actually, coming off the bay. And I think if you can do something for us, we'll all get out alive before we freeze or starve to death. So thanks a lot, Dark Cloud. This is Steve Forrester, signing off."

The steady beams of the flashlights between us made our situation less gloomy. Maybe the batteries would hold up until something happened, I told myself. I sat still, hardly breathing. Sinbad didn't move or blink. The Sheriff and Minerva lay back tired. Waldorf was asleep

or unconscious. I heard the breakers off Jonah's Bay
tumbling softly on the shore. Far away, I heard the
distant sound of foghorns and ship bells way off on
the Sound. Water dripped slowly somewhere in the
cave.

The wind began to rise. It reached a whistling, keening pitch and then I heard the distant rumble of
thunder. I sat tight, the hair prickling on the back of
my neck. I had my eyes tightly closed and sensed a
glaring flash of lightning through the rock fissure.

The wind rose to a shriek, with the deep booming
sound of thunder on its heels. There was a blinding,
crackling flash just outside. I jerked, Minerva yelped.

"Cool it," her father murmured. "Just a little
thunder and lightning."

Sinbad wormed closer, his head on my knee. "It's
okay," I told him. "I think they're working on it."

The thunder and lightning took turns coming closer,
and then suddenly they lashed out together with one
blinding, ear-splitting effect that rocked the cave.
Shattered streaks of lightning pierced through spaces
between the rocks, illuminating the cave. Booming
thunder overhead pounded the air like giant sledge-
hammers. Sheriff Landry picked Gunther Waldorf up.
"Let's move back a little. Give that storm some room."

I said softly, "Thanks, Dark Cloud. Right on. You're
doing great."

I put all the magic stuff he gave me back in the
deerskin pouch. Then I placed it on the ground, open
to the advancing storm, hoping if any friendly spirits
were working on our case, they would recognize who

it came from. Then I moved back with Sinbad to join the others.

The wind was howling outside, and the surf began to pound the shore. Thunder boomed directly overhead, followed by three brilliant stabs of lightning. The ground shook. I could smell scorched earth and stone.

Minerva was shaking her head, wide-eyed. "I don't believe this," she said. Another bolt struck immediately, sending splintered rock fragments flying around us. Minerva ducked her head. "Wake me up when it's all over!" she yelled.

Now came the tide, the awesome sound of great waves crashing higher and higher on the thin shelf of shore. The onrushing tide found the mouth of the cave. Water splashed in, the cold spumy spray soaking us.

There was a lull overhead and I could feel the pressure building. The air crackled. More water crashed against the giant rocks, splashing inside. The rocks moved, began to jiggle loose. And now the lightning struck once more, savagely, as if to get this job over and done with. *CRASH!* I felt my hair on end from the electricity in the air, and then I saw the great jagged fissure the last bolt had seared through the rock, sawing it in half.

Minerva was on her feet. By the light of the flashes, I could see her face, pale and wet, her hair damp and hanging straight down. Her eyes were glowing with excitement. "It broke the rocks! The tide is dragging them away!"

Moonlight filtered inside. The tidal waves came up

to the mouth of the cave, crashed against the rocks, and fell back, sucking away the packed earth and shattered boulders. More and more space appeared, as each advancing wave pulled back a little more of the blocked entrance to the cave with it.

Sheriff Landry was on his feet, rubbing his hands together. "I think we can do something on our own now," he said.

I jumped to help him straining against the pile of rocks still blocking the entrance. Minerva got into the act, too, pushing with all her might. The water sucked under the rocks, and suddenly the biggest one tumbled aside.

Minerva shook her fist. "Let's hear it for people power!"

I picked up the soaked spirit bag. "Thanks, Dark Cloud," I whispered. The wind lessened as we made our way through the rubble outside. The waves fell back, the tide slackened off. Water lapped at the shore, soft breakers rolled in.

The sky sparkled with a million diamonds. The moon rode alone without a cloud near it. Sinbad, barking happily, charged into the water as if challenging the receding waves. He splashed out running in and out around my feet.

Sheriff Landry carried Gunther Waldorf over his shoulder. His free hand rested on my arm, and I looked up at him. He was relaxed, his face showing the kind of warmth I had never seen.

"The next time I chew you out about anything," he

said, "I'd appreciate it if you would remind me about what happened here tonight. Okay?"

I shrugged, showing him the buckskin. "I didn't do anything. That was Dark Cloud's magic, Sheriff."

Minerva shook her head and tugged at her father's sleeve. "Hey, Pop, you better do something. He really believes that."

Sheriff Landry looked down at her, then at me. "Well, I'll tell you something. If you two ever get married, you better be careful. Steve's got some powerful friends in high places."

"Oh, blah," she said. "It was just a big storm."

I looked back at the mouth of the cave. The rocks were strewn around, broken into jagged pieces. Water swirled around. I grinned. "It sure was," I said.

Minerva, running happily on the beach, tripped. On her hands and knees, she seemed to be studying what she had fallen over. "Hey, look at this," she said.

She dug something out of the wet sand and held it in her hands. When I got closer, she tossed it to me. When I saw what it was, I nearly dropped it.

It was a bleached skull!

"Terrific, Minerva!" I said. "Now I know this is the old pirate cave my ghost was talking about."

"How do you know that?" she said. "It's just an old skull."

"Sure. But this must have been buried deep and it took all that water to flush it out. I bet it's one of the old pirate crew."

"It could have been anybody, dumbbell," she said.

"It could have been an Indian or an early settler, or anybody."

"Maybe," I said, "but I'm putting it back." She watched as I stuck it back in the soft sand, and then arranged some small stones around it.

"What are you doing that for?" she said.

"When I come back for the ghost's gold. X marks the spot."

"You're crazy. It's just an old skull," she said.

I was shaking my head, feeling good about everything, when suddenly I had the grisly thought that this skull could be that of the ghost, Captain Marion. He was killed at the site of the treasure, he had said. I shivered. I didn't want to think about that.

Minerva was waiting. "I guess you're right, Minerva. It's just an old skull," I said.

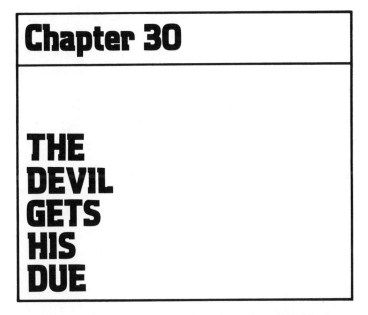

Chapter 30

THE
DEVIL
GETS
HIS
DUE

The next problem was getting Gunther Waldorf up
from the beach to a hospital. Minerva and Sinbad
solved that. Running around, they found steps that had
been cut out leading from the sandy beach shelf to the
high bluff above. Minerva had Sinbad back on his strong
chain leash, and he pulled her up the steep incline without her having to do much more than just hold on.
Waldorf had regained consciousness but was unable
to walk, so Sheriff Landry and I carried him up.

As we neared the top, I said, "You know, Sheriff,
all that beachfront and maybe part of the cave we
were in, all the way out there to Captain Billy Murdock's castle and his Jonah Jaws cave, still belongs to
Mrs. Teska. I saved her from giving it away to that
creep Yerkos."

He grimaced. "You mean, according to that scrap of paper your ghost allegedly snatched out of her hand before she had completed the formal property rights assignment to Yerkos and signed it?"

"Well, sure."

He snorted, grunting under Waldorf's weight. "Don't count your chickens before they're hatched. As I recall your story, you left the premises at that point."

"So what?" I said.

"So this. You don't know whether or not Yerkos gave her another piece of paper afterward, to get the whole deed down again in black and white. You were gone, out of there, and for all you know didn't stop anything."

I had a sinking feeling, wondering if he was right. "Holy mackerel," I said. "Gee, I guess that's possible."

"Don't let it eat at you," he said. "We'll find out soon enough. If all that property is what Big Nick Murdock left her, maybe his lawyer Gideon Pickering can stall the deed assignment while we prove Yerkos guilty of extortion."

"Well, what if you can't prove anything?"

Minerva appeared suddenly at the top of the bluff before he could answer. She was waving her arms excitedly. "Hurry up, Pop—you're missing the big fire!"

Sheriff Landry looked at me, genuinely surprised. "That's one on me, all right. I forgot all about it."

I smelled smoke then, and we both hurried Waldorf up the remaining steps. Flames were shooting up from a dense pall of smoke. I had forgotten, along with the Sheriff, about the fire in the old prayer room of the

King Dick house. The entire street of Hellsfire was choked with fire trucks and police cars.

I laughed and Sheriff Landry shot me a dirty look. "What's so funny?"

I shrugged. "A fire on Hellsfire," I said.

Firemen were playing their hoses on the shooting flames. The old Colonial looked nearly gone. The roof and two walls had fallen. The rest looked charred and gutted.

A policeman saw us, yelled something, and a patrol car, its red domelight spinning, broke away and zoomed up to us. I knew the driver, Sergeant Sweeney. He and the other cop with him got out, and helped Sheriff Landry put Gunther Waldorf into the car. "We'll need an ambulance for this man," Sheriff Landry said, "or have to get him to the hospital ourselves."

Sweeney stared at Sheriff Landry's smoke-grimed face. "What happened to you? Don't tell me you were in there?"

The Chief shrugged. "Yes, but we got out another way. What happened here?"

Sergeant Sweeney shook his head. "The firemen found three people alive in there. We got an ambulance for them and rushed them off."

"Three?"

Sweeney nodded. "Yeah, Chief. A man and a woman —one was the guy who resided here—name of Yerkos— and the other man—" He broke off and stared down at Gunther Waldorf lying on the back seat. "I'm seeing double. This guy is him!"

"Call it a close resemblance," the Sheriff said. "Any idea who the woman was, Sweeney?"

The sarge shook his head. "We got her down as an unidentified female. The other guy—"

"What happened to them?" the Sheriff asked. "Burned in the fire?"

"No," Sweeney said. "Smoke inhalation."

I cut in excitedly. "It wasn't Mrs. Teska, was it?"

Sweeney grinned down at me. "The old lady down Steamboat Road? Nah—what would she be doing here? This was a young woman—"

"Sister Sofi's spirit," I said.

Sweeney's jaw dropped. "Huh?"

Sheriff Landry dropped his hand on my shoulder and I got the message, to butt out. "What about Yerkos?"

Sweeney shook his head. "Now, that was real weird, Chief. What happened to him, I mean. He was outside, when we pulled up, home free. Then suddenly he remembered something he left inside. He rushed inside to get it, right through the flames. Now guess what?"

The Sheriff looked at him stonily. "You tell me."

"He was coming out, waving something in his hand, saying he was rich, that he had a million dollars—when a big beam from the overhang fell on him." Sweeney shook his head. "I doubt if that man will ever walk again."

"What was in his hand?"

Sweeney grinned. "I thought you might be interested in that, Chief." His hand dug into his pocket and came out holding a thin pink slip of paper. He opened it and read from it. "It says right here, Chief, one million dollars, pay to the order of Solo Yerkos."

Sheriff Landry held out his hand. "Better let me have that." He looked closely at it, nodded, then showed it to me. "Guess you were right about that one, too, Steve. I owe you an apology."

The check was signed by Mrs. Anna Teska. Made out, like Sweeney said, for a million dollars.

"Good deal," I said. "Maybe we ought to head over to her house now, Sheriff, before it's too late. Just in case."

He looked down at me coldly. "Too late for what?"

"Well, you know, she believed all that junk. If Yerkos got her to sign the check, she might have made up her mind to join her dead sister Sofi."

Sweeney stared puzzled, and cocked his head at me. Sheriff Landry didn't jump for his car like I expected. "Here we go again. Sounds like you're up to your old scare tactics."

"No, honest, Sheriff," I said. "She showed me a picture of the tombstone she ordered. She told me she's got a brand-new coffin in her bedroom." He continued to look down at me, as if debating with himself whether or not he should take another chance with me.

"Besides," I said, "you got to take Minerva home anyway. And Mrs. Teska is practically on your way."

Sheriff Landry heaved his shoulders, and let them drop with a long resigned sigh. "Okay, let's go. Get in the car."

We followed him to the old Pontiac, and as he slid behind the wheel, he turned to me. "If this turns out to be a wild goose chase, I take back every nice thing I said about you tonight."

I shrugged and looked at Minerva. "What do you think?"

Minerva tossed her head. "I think you're crazy, as usual. Besides, you're getting all the credit, and I'm the one who went through all that garbage."

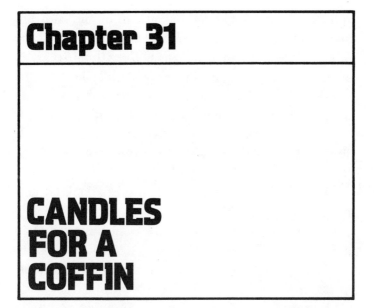

Chapter 31

CANDLES FOR A COFFIN

Like the boy in the old story who cried wolf once too often, I was having the same problem with Sheriff Landry taking me seriously. He had known me too long, and been faked out by too many of my imaginative leaps to exaggerated conclusions. Even though I was on a hot hitting streak this night, he must have figured that a lot of it was just dumb luck. So it was only natural for him to regard my worrying over Mrs. Teska as a return to form, getting excited over nothing.

He didn't race his old souped-up Pontiac out to Mrs. Teska's like a kamikaze daredevil. Instead he stopped for all the red lights like a law-abiding citizen, not like a cop going all out to handle an emergency.

When we got to her place, the clock on his dashboard was past midnight. Her lights were out, upstairs and down. Sheriff Landry wheeled in at the curb but instead of cutting off his engine, and jumping out, he just sat there, the motor idling. "Everything seems in order," he said. "I forget why we're here. Tell me again."

"Well, Sheriff, when I left the seance, she was getting ready to die to meet her sister Sofi's spirit."

He stifled a yawn. "Well, I've got the check back, and you told me your ghost scared the spirit off. Maybe that ended it for Mrs. Teska."

"Maybe," I said. "But I want to take a look upstairs to be sure, Sheriff."

He shrugged. "Okay, but make it snappy. We've all had a hard night, and I've got a tough day ahead."

Minerva got out of the car with me. "I'll come along, in case you need a witness that she's dying."

"Very funny, Minerva," I said. "Okay, come on."

Sinbad jumped out of the car and we ran up the side steps. I knew Mrs. Teska went to bed early, and wondered how I was going to wake her up to find out if she was still okay, and not trying to die, or anything.

Sinbad solved that problem. He sniffed, scratching at the door and whining. I leaned over the side rail and saw her window blinds were drawn, her windows closed.

I knocked softly. "Mrs. Teska," I whispered, "are you all right?" I jiggled the knob. "Mrs. Teska," I called louder. The door was locked.

Sinbad had his nose at the crack under the door. He sniffed and sneezed, backed up whining, and looked up at the locked door. A deep growl rumbled in his chest. "Hey, what's wrong?" I asked him. He looked up at me, growled, and clawed at the door. "I think she's sleeping," I told him. "I'm not sure if waking her up is such a hot idea. It's kind of late."

Sinbad made the cracked parrot sound, flattened himself at the crack again, sniffing. His ears twitched, and he backed off, whimpering. He shook his big head then, and growling fiercely, rammed into the door, hitting it hard. He growled and butted it again.

Sheriff Landry called from the street below. "What's wrong?"

"I don't know," I said. I got down next to Sinbad, and tried to smell what was bothering him. A heavy sweet odor came from inside. I yelled. "It's a funny smell, Sheriff. Like gas. You better come up."

He came running and put his nose down to the bottom of the door. He got up, looking at the side windows. "You know where she keeps her key, Steve?"

I ran to the special stone where she hid her spare key, and turned it over. "It's not here," I said.

The Sheriff lunged at the door, battering it with his shoulder. The hinges gave, and he knocked it open. We rushed in, before he could stop us. "Hold it, kids," he yelled. "It's cyanide gas."

Sinbad had already charged through, barking furiously and heading across her living room. The Sheriff began opening the windows, and the blinds. Minerva and I ran to the other side, doing the same. The odor was making me nauseous. Holding my breath, I ran to the kitchen. To my surprise the gas jets were all turned to the "off" position. I ran back to the Sheriff, sucking in some air at the first window. "It's not kitchen gas," I told him. He was nodding as if he already knew, and heading for her bedroom.

Sinbad and Minerva were already there. Sinbad was barking up a storm. Minerva stood pointing, her jaw hanging.

"Weirdsville," she muttered.

Instead of her bed, a big coffin filled the center of Mrs. Teska's bedroom. Set on the floor all around it were long black candles, flickering and burning. The moonlight streaming in made the whole scene seem spooky and unreal.

I yelled, "Mrs. Teska, where are you?" More dark lit candles smelling like flowers were on end tables at either side of the coffin. Sinbad was whining, trying to jump into the coffin. I looked over the side.

Her eyes were closed. She lay there fully dressed.

"Mrs. Teska," I yelled, "holy mackerel, what are you doing in your coffin? You're not supposed to be dead yet."

Sheriff Landry was sweeping up the candles, dashing them to the floor, stepping on the flames. Minerva was doing the same to those already burning on the floor.

The Sheriff knocked a window out and a cold blast of air swept across the room. "Let's get her up, if we can."

I shook her shoulder. Her eyes opened sleepily. "What?"

"Wake up, Mrs. Teska," I said, shaking her some more. "I think you got a gas leak here someplace."

She blinked, then coughed. "Is no more gas, Stevie. I already shut off."

I went to the phone. "I guess I better call a doctor, huh, Sheriff?" Before he could answer, she said drowsily, "Is no more phone. I shut off everything."

I stared at her. "Gee, you really believed that guy! I'm surprised at you, Mrs. Teska. You were really getting ready to die tonight, weren't you?"

She looked up at me, annoyed rather than grateful. "Is my business," she said.

Sheriff Landry leaned over the coffin. He held one of the snuffed-out black candles close to her face. "Mrs. Teska, where did you get these candles?"

The old lady coughed and I patted her back. "From nice man Solo Yerkos. He say is best to have burning when this old lady make ready to meet sister Sofi spirit. Is nice smell, like flowers, no?"

Sheriff Landry leaned over and began hauling her out. "You better get out of there and near a window with some fresh air. Those candles are poison. Potassium cyanide crystals."

We got her out of the coffin to the window, and the Sheriff insisted she keep walking and inhaling more fresh air. "What you talking, poison?" she said to the Sheriff, annoyed with him too.

"One of the deadliest known, Mrs. Teska. It's the same kind used in fumigating houses."

"From candles?" she said, puzzled.

He picked up one and broke it open. "Special candles, I'm afraid. Potassium cyanide crystals are inserted. With the heat it expands to prussic acid and then hydrocyanic-acid gas, one of the deadliest poisons known. It doesn't take very long to paralyze the breathing center in your brain. If it weren't for your friend Steve, here, you might have been dead by now."

She looked at him, still annoyed. "You no understand, Mister Sheriff. Is what Mrs. Teska is supposed to do. For to meet sister Sofi. Sofi spirit say to get ready to die."

"That wasn't your sister Sofi's spirit, Mrs. Teska. The whole thing there was a fake," I said.

She bristled angrily. "You nice boy, Stevie, but you not friend to say that. How you know what you say, little boy?"

"Listen, Mrs. Teska," I said. "About how long is it since you saw your sister Sofi?"

She shrugged. "Oh, long time. When children. Maybe fifty, maybe better sixty year ago."

"Back in the old country?"

"Well, for sure. In Serbia."

"You've been here since you were a young girl, right, about eighteen or twenty, and Sofi never came over. Right?"

"For sure, Stevie. Is right. Sofi never come."

"Did you know how to speak English back in the old country?"

She shook her head. "No, silly boy. No speak then but learn here. Still not speak too good, you know."

"Okay. You told me Sofi died when she was young, right?"

She nodded. "Yes, very young girl."

"So when did she learn how to speak English?"

She stared, shaken. "What you say?"

"That voice she was talking to you with—her spirit voice—she was talking to you in English, remember. Very good English, too, better than you speak, right?"

She was silent, thinking. "How you know this?"

"I was down in the basement there, listening. I heard her."

She began to cross herself, swaying from side to side. "Oh, Stevie, what very big fool old Mrs. Teska be."

Sheriff Landry leaned over and put something into her hand. She looked up at him. "What this?" He smiled. "You tell me." She looked at it closely, the pink check she had made out to Yerkos. "Is more foolishness," she said, and tore it into small pieces.

She took my hand and held it close to her. "You good boy, Stevie. You no let Mrs. Teska stay big fool."

"Well, that's okay," I said. "But besides that check for a million dollars you got back, you also didn't lose your beach property, you know. You never got to sign that piece of paper. I got it someplace." I went through my pockets and couldn't find it. The sheriff grinned, dug into his pocket, and handed it to me. I gave it to Mrs. Teska.

She looked at it dazed. "How you get this?"

I nearly laughed. "From a friend of mine."

She crossed herself again. She walked over to her old rocking chair and began to rock back and forth. "Funny thing if Mrs. Teska not have to die now."

"I told you," I said, "you probably got another twenty years."

She smiled. "No matter. Anyway, Mrs. Teska she not be in such a hurry now."

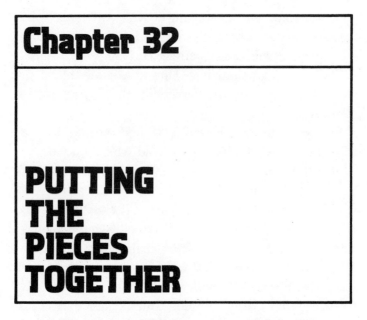

Chapter 32

PUTTING THE PIECES TOGETHER

We were in the Sheriff's souped-up old Pontiac again. He glanced at me. "Well, that's two out of two you've got. I suppose you want it all—three out of three."

"How do you mean?" I said.

"You were right about Gunther Waldorf being kidnapped. You were right about Mrs. Teska being duped by Solo Yerkos. All that's left is proving the new Citizens' Committee is the crooked bunch you said they were from the beginning."

"Well, I heard a little of it at that meeting over at Solo Yerkos's house. But how are we going to prove it?"

"We have three of the principals at the hospital," he said. "Yerkos, Simpson, and the mystery woman who came out of the house with them when it caught on fire."

"She's no mystery woman," I said. "She's got to be

the one pretending to be Mrs. Teska's sister Sofi's spirit."

"How did she do that?" Minerva asked.

"You never actually saw her, Minerva," I said. "It was a shape or shadow behind a light screen or curtain. Maybe gauze, or transparent anyway. It was lit up and her shadow was moving behind it."

"How do you know?" she said. "You're guessing. You never looked behind it."

"Well, sure, but it figured they had some strong light behind there, projecting her image on the screen. She would move closer or back, to make her image bigger or smaller. Maybe they had a fan back there, too, stirring up the air to move the curtain and make it spooky. Or maybe a wind machine."

"I wish I'd been there," Minerva said. "What about her voice? What did she sound like?"

"I can't imitate her little girl voice. It was spooky, a real good impersonation of a nice young spirit. But her mistake was her English was too good."

"She must have been an actress that they hired?"

"I guess so. Maybe like that guy Simpson who took the part of Gunther Waldorf. He sure was a good actor."

Sheriff Landry put the Pontiac into overdrive. "We'll find out all the facts pretty soon."

The village streets were deserted as we zoomed down Steamboat Road. Something still bothered me. "You know, Sheriff, Mr. Gideon Pickering told me that he and Mr. Calloway were the trustees for Mrs. Teska's estate. So how come Calloway was at that meeting, in with those crooks?"

"I don't understand that myself," the Sheriff said.

"E. Biggs Calloway is too old and respected to get himself involved with that nonsense."

I asked how old.

"Over seventy, maybe pushing eighty, I guess," he said.

"This Calloway wasn't that old. Short, fat, and chunky. Reddish hair. About your age, Sheriff, or my pop's."

"Oh, that would be Chester Calloway, the old man's son. He's in real estate, promoting land scheme investments, a lot of things. The get-rich-quick type."

"That sounds like him."

"There was a big guy, you said. Man called Joe?"

"Yeah. He looked like a pro linebacker."

"Sounds like Joe Case. Brad's big brother."

I was surprised. "You know him?"

"We went to school together. Had a few run-ins down through the years. Joe isn't too bright but carries a grudge pretty well."

"I still don't understand why they kidnapped Gunther Waldorf in the first place," Minerva said. "It sure sounds like a dumb plan to me."

"It was about some secret study he made of the Shinnecock reservation land, Minerva," I said. "They hoped he would tell them there was enough oil there so they could find some excuse to get a government lease to drill there."

"That's dumb, too. If they had any oil, the Shinnecocks would drill for it themselves. They could use the money."

"That's it!" I yelled. "They had a hunch that would happen, I bet, and wanted to beat the Indians to it."

"Oh, blah," Minerva said. "Me and my big mouth. What do you think, Pop?"

He braked and turned into a driveway. "Maybe we'll find out now. We're at the hospital."

We went in and found cops all over the place. Sheriff Landry went over to talk to them, came back, and told us to find a couple of chairs and wait. He thumbed over his shoulder to the big cop, Sweeney. "According to Sergeant Sweeney, they're all scared. Maybe I can get a confession out of them."

"Don't forget to read them their rights first," I said.

He looked down at me sourly. "How's that?"

I hugged Sinbad tightly. "We don't want to lose this case and have it thrown out of court."

"Oh, brother," he said. "I don't think I'm going to like having you around for a son-in-law."

"Well, I heard about those things," I said.

"I don't think I want to marry him ever anyway, Pop," Minerva said. "He's so lucky, he makes me sick."

Her old man waved and turned away. "Stick around. You might get sicker."

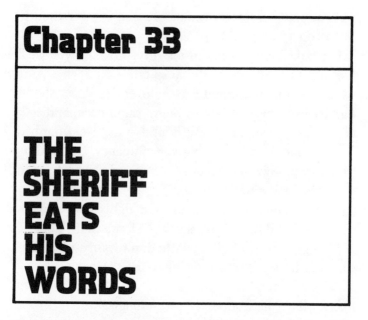

Chapter 33

THE SHERIFF EATS HIS WORDS

Confessions take forever. We didn't get back to the Sheriff's house until nearly three o'clock in the morning. All the excitement had worn off, and I was tired and sleepy. Sinbad had had it, too, and was snoozing away on the floor, his muzzle resting on Minerva Landry's feet.

The Sheriff had fixed us all something to eat. He knew what Sinbad liked and, as usual, had plenty of dog food around. Now we were in the den in front of the fireplace. The fire crackled and the flames leaped and danced around, but this time a fire was relaxing to watch.

He lit up his pipe, puffed contentedly for a while, and then took out his old black notebook. "Well, the confessions went down to headquarters, but I've got some notes here in case you're interested."

"They all confessed?" I said, surprised.

"Simpson cracked first. He didn't know Gunther Waldorf had escaped the basement fire, and didn't want to be an accessory to murder. Then Mrs. Simpson confessed. She was frightened, too."

Minerva punched my arm. "Mrs. Simpson?"

He nodded, reading from the notebook. "Louise and Waldo Simpson. Small-time theatrical team. She's a singer. He does pantomime and impersonations. Not too successful here, and they work mostly in clubs in South America and Europe. At one stage in his life, Solo Yerkos worked an act as a stage magician and hypnotist. They're old friends, and Yerkos figured he would get them a few weeks' work and some good money when he was called in on this deal. Mrs. Simpson didn't do too much during the seance with Mrs. Teska, but she admitted being prepared to make another appearance at the old lady's house, in case she didn't go along with the idea of dying sooner."

"You mean like a spirit or ghost?"

"Something like that. She has the trained voice for it."

"Yerkos confessed too, Pop?" Minerva asked.

"He had to once we showed him the other confessions. That's when he dumped it all on Calloway and Joe Case. They originated the scheme."

"But they haven't confessed?" I said.

"No, we haven't picked them up yet or charged them. But I imagine Brad will crack first. He's a decent guy, not like his brother, and I don't think he liked any part of this. They most likely sold him a bill of goods, and then his big brother always dominated Brad."

"What about Gunther Waldorf—the real one?"

Sheriff Landry tamped his pipe out and closed the book. "Incredible, but you were right on that one, too, up to and including your last guess about the Shinnecock oil deposits. He did the study as a favor to the Indians, and it was supposed to be a secret. The Shinnecock leaders and Mr. Waldorf were well aware of how greedy interests might try to take over their rights if the news got out."

"Is he okay now?"

"A little weak, but coming out of it. The docs are getting rid of the drugs in his system, and his mind seems clear enough already." He filled his pipe again, and lit up. "I've got to give you credit, Steve. You got them all."

Minerva tossed her long blond hair. "Oh, blah! He keeps getting all the credit. I knew the new Waldorf over at the house was a phony, and I could prove it before anybody knew it."

Sheriff Landry looked at her. "Prove it, you said? How?"

"From the time you went there and got him to autograph that book for me."

Her pop looked puzzled. "I don't get it."

She went to the bookcase, came back with the paperback, handed it to him, and flounced back on the sofa. "It's all there, right on the inside front page. You saw it and Steve saw it. I was the only one who knew it."

Sheriff Landry looked at the book and after a while began laughing. "Good girl," he said.

I stuck out my hand. "Can I see it?" He tossed it over and I looked at the inscription. Finally I had to shake my head. "I don't get it," I said.

To

Minerva Landry
with best wishes,
Gunter Waldorf

Minerva hooted. She pointed to the inscription. "He spelled his name wrong, dumbbell. He didn't even know how to spell his own name."

I still was puzzled. "Huh?"

"He left out the 'h,'" she said laughing. "And you think you're such a great detective."

Sheriff Landry got back his usual grim look. "Well, you had something there, Minerva. Why didn't you tell me?"

"Oh, blah," she said. "You never believe anybody. Besides, I figured I would crack this whole case open by myself, and then you would have to pay attention."

Sheriff Landry scratched his head. "Well, I heard about your checking out the garbage. That's real good detective work, Minerva, and I want to give you credit for it."

I nodded. "That really was good thinking, Minerva. I never thought of doing that."

"Well, you thought about nearly everything else," the Sheriff said. "I admit now I was wrong, and I'm willing to eat my words."

"Well," I said, looking at him.

"What's bugging you now?" he said testily.

"I thought it was more like you were going to eat that thing outside. Remember—that poster of Brad Case for sheriff?"

He stared hard at me.

I shrugged. "It's okay. If you don't exactly feel like doing that, I'll make another deal with you."

"Like what?"

"Well, my mom went away to meet Pop out there in Montauk. And Sinbad and I are alone. Also I'm tired and this looks like a good warm place to spend the rest of the night."

Sheriff Landry smiled, rubbing his hands. "It's a deal." He looked sharply at me. "Any other reason?"

"Well, only one more. I kind of expect that pirate ghost to come back and remind me of my bargain to help him find his gold. I've had enough excitement tonight."

Sheriff Landry stood up. "I'll get some more pillows and blankets."

"Tomorrow ought to be a good day for it," I said. He waited. "No school," I said.

He went out scratching his head.

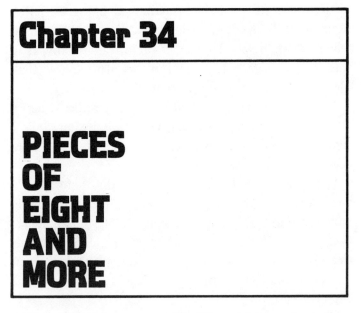

Chapter 34

PIECES OF EIGHT AND MORE

"Remember," Minerva said, "I'm only coming along for the laughs. I still don't believe your story about that pirate gold and your ghost."

"Maybe you shouldn't have come along," I said. "We'll have to go into that cave again. It might be dangerous."

"Dangerous?" Minerva laughed. "Where were you last night? Who was fighting the fire while you were playing with your Indian bones and beads? Who found the sliding panel that got us out of there? Who led the way through the cave with Sinbad and fell down the first big drop while you guys were way back waiting for me to find the way out?"

"Well," I said, "your pop and I were carrying Gunther Waldorf. We couldn't walk any faster."

"Faster?" she hooted. "You moved like snails. But besides all that, dumbbell, you still wouldn't know where the gold was, I mean, if there really is any, if it wasn't for me, would you? I mean, who found that old skull, or did you forget that, too?"

I turned to Herky, who had been silent while Minerva and I went through our usual type of discussion. "She's right, Herk. More or less, that is. Anyway, she did find the skull, that's a fact."

Herky smiled. "I've been through this before with you guys. And while I don't necessarily agree with Minerva that your ghost is a figment of your imagination, I'm really looking forward to searching for the treasure. It would substantiate your story, for one thing."

"Name another thing, Herk, before I fall asleep," Minerva said.

Herky shrugged his thin shoulders. "Well, just think! If it's there, we would be bringing together two disparate things—the supernatural event of the ghost, and the reality of the gold."

Minerva tossed her long hair. "Oh, blah! I thought you were intelligent. Now you're sounding just as nutty as Steve."

Herky smiled tolerantly. He knows Minerva tries to act dumb and pooh-poohs brains, even though she's almost as smart as he is. "Let's consider it just a theory waiting to be resolved. We'll know considerably more about fact versus fiction when we investigate the cave itself."

Sinbad didn't say anything. He just chugged along, low to the ground, his dark muzzle sniffing the strange scents along the beach, as we got closer to the cave area below Hellsfire Street. The sand and water always excited him, but on this morning he seemed more responsive than usual, as if he realized how important that search was for me and him, the last hope of the pirate ghost to get what he considered rightfully his.

Sheriff Landry had been a good sport after breakfast. He had some things to do down at his office but he knew Minerva and I had a school holiday. When he asked our plans for the day, I said I was going back to the cave to hunt for the gold. He scratched his head, and looked at his daughter.

"I'll go along, too, Pop," Minerva said. "Just for the laughs, you understand. I don't believe that story of Steve and his ghost any more than you do."

"There's just one more problem about it, Sheriff," I said. "I'd like Herky Krakower to come along. If we did find anything, he'd be able to tell us if it was valuable or not."

The Sheriff shrugged good-naturedly. "Seems sensible. I'd go along with anything Herky says. What's the problem?"

I reminded him about how Herky didn't walk too good, and it was a long walk from the Sheriff's house to the cave, even if Herky's mom drove him over. I didn't know if she would be able to take us all to the Hellsfire section, considering the fire there, the conditions, and so on.

The Sheriff wolfed down the last of his bacon, eggs, and toast. "No problem," he said, pointing toward the phone. "Get him on the horn and ready in fifteen minutes. I'll pick him up and take you all over myself. I'd like to check the house anyway, for the records."

"Thanks, Sheriff. It would be terrific for Herky's adventurous spirit, too, you know."

"So you tell me," he said. "If he doesn't come out of there with a broken leg, I'll say you were right again."

Herky sounded thrilled to be asked along. Sheriff Landry picked him up and promised Mrs. Krakower he would bring Herky back later. With Herky, Sinbad, and Minerva—all old friends, it looked like the start of a nice, happy adventure.

The Sheriff dropped us off at the bluff edge on Hellsfire. The old Garrison Colonial was as good as gone. Only a charred wall was standing, still smoldering. I had forgotten to tell Sheriff Landry about the Lincoln with the same scratch on the fender. It was just as well I kept my mouth shut. We passed it in the driveway, a burned-out wreck you could hardly identify as a Lincoln, let alone one with a scratched fender.

When the Sheriff let us off, he advised us to be careful. The storm might have weakened some of the cave wall or ceiling, and he didn't feel much like coming by later to dig us out. "Don't worry," I said. "When we find the gold, we'll all be walking two feet off the ground."

"Well, that's another thing," he said. "Technically, I hope you realize, all that treasure, if there is any, belongs to Mrs. Teska, considering it might be found on her property."

Minerva took over. She put her hands on her hips.

"Don't embarrass me in front of my friends, Pop. Let's everybody pretend he didn't say that."

Sheriff Landry put his hands up, smiling. "Well, it was a thought."

Minerva sniffed. "So *you* say. Let's go, guys."

Herky hesitated. He looked up at Sheriff Landry shyly. "I don't mean to contradict you, Sheriff Landry—"

The Sheriff nodded pleasantly. "Go ahead, son. Anything you have to say."

"It's just that the ghost—assuming he is real—has already established a priority claim to the treasure. We're talking of something placed in the cave about two hundred years ago. If he can identify it, I doubt that any court of law—"

Sheriff Landry smiled. "As usual, you're right, Herky. I hadn't considered the priority claim." He waved his hands. "As Minerva said, forget I mentioned it. Go on and have a good dig down there."

So we regrouped and went down the steps to the beach. Herky was a little slow but wasn't holding us up that much. The cave looked less frightening in daylight. The effects of the storm were everywhere, rocks and boulders strewn around as if a giant hand had wanted to create a different-looking beach.

"I'm glad you wanted to come along, Herk," I said. "With your knowledge of old coins, we'll have a good idea of how much the pirate treasure is worth when we find it."

Herky laughed. "You mean, if we find it. There's a

good chance the tides washed it out to sea long ago, Steve."

Minerva ran ahead when we neared the skull and picked it up to show Herky. "I found this just as we were getting out of the cave. Do you think it might belong to that crazy ghost who claims he was killed here, at the site of the treasure?"

Herky examined the skull from all angles. "There's no evidence of skull damage. Did your ghost tell you how he was killed, Steve? Head bashed in, or shot?"

"He didn't mention that," I said. "He wears a bandage over one eye, if that's any help."

Herky set the skull down among the stones on the sand. "Well, out of curiosity, you might ask him next time around. I've read that pirates usually killed the seamen who helped bury their treasure. That way there would be fewer to remember where it was. And they had another reason, the superstitious belief that the dead man would guard the buried treasure. His ghostly spirit would drive all intruders away."

We followed a path through the rubble into the cave, where the bed rose steeply. Pointing to the rise, I said, "That pirate Captain Bones who had it buried knew what he was doing. It's all uphill, and curving from here on. The entrance was blocked off with stones so big, three of us couldn't budge them.

"I forgot to tell you, Herk, that you're in for your share if we find the pirate chest and bring it back to Captain Marion, the ghost. I bet he'll give us a big tip, and Minerva, you and I will all be rich."

Minerva held her ears. "Don't listen, he'll drive you crazy."

"Well, Steve, don't get your hopes too high," Herky said. "There may be gold doubloons and guineas, but the Spanish galleons of that day carried mostly silver."

"What about those pieces of eight? I read that pirates used them."

Herky nodded, as we stepped carefully around the rocks tumbled around the mouth of the cave. "The silver Eight Reales, *pesos de ocho*. That was silver; consider it like a dollar. Sometimes the *real* was divided into eight parts to make change. One piece was called a 'bit.' Each equaled twelve and a half cents. That's the origin of the phrase two bits for a quarter. Or it was divided into quarters or halves. All 'bits.'

"It came into the Virginia colony and the Massachusetts colony because of clandestine trade with New Spain and the pirate raids on its ports. It was basic currency for the early American settler."

Minerva forgot she didn't believe in the treasure. "How much would they be worth today, Herk?"

"About ten dollars."

She nodded. "Not bad if we find a bunch."

"There could be other treasure, you know," Herk said. "Taken in booty, rings, bracelets, gold earrings. And the precious stones—diamonds, rubies, and emeralds."

Minerva faced me. "Okay, you give the ghost the gold. Herky and I will stick with the diamonds and emeralds."

"Fat chance, Minerva," I said. "You're forgetting I got this ghost haunting me. That's all I need to do now is cheat him. Forget it. He gets everything we find, and it's up to him to reward us any way he wants."

Herky was wagging his head. "But on the other hand, the fancied gold pieces may be only bronze coins, the jewelry fake, and the stones only imitation glass."

"Don't be a defeatist, Herk. I'm trying to think positive." I waved the big sack I held for carrying the treasure back. "I'm only going by what the pirate ghost said. He said he wanted his gold that they cheated him out of. So he ought to know."

"Perhaps," Herky said. "But it's likely that he never saw the booty, and only assumed it was gold. Anyway, it's all academic if we don't find it."

I flashed my light around the walls. "We got to find it. He's so sure of where it is. He's awfully tired and doesn't have much energy. I'd hate to disappoint him."

Herky tugged my arm and pointed toward the opposite end of the cave. Sinbad was sniffing the ground excitedly, going around in circles. "It looks as if Sinbad found something, Steve."

Minerva shrieked and ran over. "That better not be a bone, Sinbad," she said warningly to him, "or you'll be off my list of friends."

There was a wide ledge under the slanted roof of the cave. We were a short distance from the entrance, in a high recess of ridged rock and clay. Sinbad's big feet were flying like scoops as he dislodged the loose top clay and dirt. Suddenly the entire side of the ledge caved in, and Sinbad jumped back and looked up, surprised.

"I think you got it," I told him. "Now it's time for me and my shovel."

Herky was studying the cave walk, some of the loose dirt. "The pirate who buried it here had a system. He put the treasure above ground. This ledge is safely over the water line even at high tide. He wasn't taking any chances of having his booty washed out to sea."

I dug and dumped a half dozen shovels' worth, and kept on digging. There was a rasping metallic sound as my shovel hit something hard. I looked at Minerva.

She screamed, happily clapping her hands. "Don't stop, dumbbell, you hit something."

Herky's eyes were sparkling. He tried to hide his own excitement by sounding cool. "I think that's the sound a treasure chest makes when contacted properly."

"Hold the light closer, Minerva," I said, digging like crazy.

She dropped to her knees and began pushing the loose dirt away with both hands. "Herky, you hold the light. I got to do this." In another minute she looked up at me, awed and excited. "Look! There are two of them!"

The chests were old, set side by side. Both were small, about a foot high, half again as wide, nearly two feet long. We tugged them out, scraping the damp clay off. Then I noticed the lock of the first one was sprung open. I looked at Herky, a little uneasy and disappointed, worried now that somebody had somehow beaten us to it. But it had felt very heavy as I pulled it out.

The lid snapped back easily. The chest smelled moldy, an awful mildewed odor. Minerva was already digging her hands in.

"Some treasure," she wailed. "These are stones and pebbles."

I dug in with my hands, too. There was nothing but

stones. I dumped the chest over. More stones, all sizes. "When the ghost hears about this, he'll have a fit," I said.

Herky was looking intently into the hollow I had dug in the ledge. "Cheer up. Steve. The second chest might be something."

"How can you tell?"

He pointed out the timber wall that had originally been set between the chests. Mildewed and rotted, it had disintegrated. "I think the first chest was a deliberate fake," he said. "A dummy to fool whoever found it. The second chest was hidden, protected by this wall. You can see he had another layer of stones here. Time has eroded it but I think it stood up very well considering all the years."

The second padlock was still intact. I hit it a few times with my pickaxe, and the lock snapped off from its brass hasps.

"Well, here goes," I said, closing my eyes. I heard Minerva's happy shout. The open chest was a sea of sparkling stones. Green, red, orange, white, blue, yellow, and purple. I sank my hands into them. It looked like a fortune.

Minerva held the sack open and I scooped the stones out and dumped them in. "How much do you figure these precious stones are worth?" I asked Herk.

He was rubbing a small red one on a rock. As I watched, it crumbled to a dusty powder. "About five dollars," he said. "This stuff is glass."

I couldn't believe all those beautiful stones were worthless. "Boy, that pirate Captain Bones sure must have been stupid," I said. "Somebody faked him out. Are you sure this is all junk?"

Herky shrugged. "It looks to me like costume jewelry, the kind you can get at a dime store. But it was useful in those days for barter with Indians and so on. Let's see what's underneath."

The next layer was eye-boggling. The entire casket was covered with coins, silver, and gold-glittering odd-shaped pieces.

"The gold!" I yelled.

"Sorry, Steve, those are bronze."

"Herky," I said, "you're a real killjoy. If you don't say one of these is gold, next time I'm leaving you out of my treasure hunt."

He smiled and picked up a small coin. "This one is worth more than gold, Steve. It's a silver tetradrachm from Thrace."

"So what? It's still only silver. I want—"

Herky turned the small coin over. "On the reverse side here is Athene, the Greek goddess. From around 300 B.C. It's the most famous coin of antiquity, Steve."

"What's it worth?"

He shrugged. "Priceless."

"Okay," I said. "Let's find more."

Minerva was hugging Sinbad. "You want to know something?" she told him. "You're going to be the richest dog in town."

Chapter 35

FAREWELL TO THE GHOST

The ghost came again exactly at midnight. I was expecting him, and when Sinbad whined I was up at once. He was hard to see, his outline wavering and his form not altogether there.

"Aye, lad," he said in a weak and listless voice, "it's the truth what yer thinkin'. There's not much energy left. So I'll ask ye just the one time, did ye find me gold?"

I hated to disappoint him on that, and I nodded yes, hoping he wouldn't get too mad. "Yeah, but the fact is, Captain Marion, there really wasn't that much gold there."

His form filled out as he bellowed, "What's that ye say?"

"Well, there was some. A few gold guineas, doubloons, and half-eagles worth about five dollars each. Some bronze coins worth about three dollars apiece." His one eye looked at me so balefully, I had to swallow hard before going on with the list and hope he wouldn't blast me before I finished. "There was a lot of Dutch, German, Austrian talers in silver, and some Spanish dollars, also in silver, the old pieces of eight worth about ten dollars each now. Plus some precious stones that only look precious. I mean, they were only junk glass—"

His form agitated, swelled, and left the ground, and he floated over the bed a few seconds. His voice was almost a shriek. "What's that yer sayin'? No gold? Are ye tellin' me Captain Bones, may his bones turn to dust, cheated me of me rightful share, after all is done?"

"Well, not exactly. According to my friend Herky, who is an expert on old coins, there was an Austrian coin from 1780. The famous Maria Theresa taler, he said, a very valuable silver dollar." He had settled down but was shaking his head, disappointed. "But also there was one special coin there from ancient Greece, from Thrace, that's the most famous coin of antiquity, he said. It should be worth a lot more than gold, Captain Marion."

The ghostly outline became clearer. "Ah, yer the good lad after all is said. Cash it in, then, and do the job ye promised to do."

I shook my head. "I don't understand."

His voice became soft. "Now yer a bright enough lad, so bear with me. What would a shade like me do with the gold if ye found it?"

"I don't know. I couldn't figure it out."

"What I want, y'see, is a proper grave."

"A proper grave?"

"Aye, laddie. To rest me bones. So I'm askin' ye now to get me a stone. With the fit and proper words writ on it. An' all to be set over me own proper grave. Can ye do it, lad, with what ye'll be gettin' for the coins?"

"Sure, I think so. Easy," I said. "No question about it. What do you want inscribed on the stone?"

He was silent a moment, thinking. Then his voice became full and stronger again. "Let it read: *Here lies John Francis Marion. May his bones rest in peace. 1760–1805.* Ye got that, lad?"

"Okay, sure. Anything else? How about some flowers?"

"That'd be real nice, matie. A loverly touch an' sentiment. See that it's done, an' one day I'll be back to visit me own fit an' proper grave. An' my thanks to ye, lad, that's a good lad, an' I bless ye for what ye done."

His form wavered as he turned away, and then he was gone. Sinbad was already asleep and snoring. It took me a little while longer, but I was smiling when hugging Sinbad, I finally drifted off. You sleep better when everything turns out all right.

Sinbad already knew that.